A Secret Baby FOR THE COWBOY

SWEET RIVER RANCH ROMANCE - BOOK 5

VALERIE COMER

GreenWords Media

I will restore to you the years
that the swarming locust has eaten…
Joel 2:25a ESV

FREE BOOK?

Love cowboys? Me, too! That's why I'd like to offer you an ebook copy of *The Cowboy's Forever Crush* free as an introduction to the world of my Montana Ranches Christian Romance series. This story world encompasses the Saddle Springs series, the Cavanagh Cowboys series, and now the Sweet River Ranch series.

Come on in and be lassoed by love!

https://valeriecomer.com/subscribe-crush

CHAPTER ONE

Bryce Sullivan hated being called into his grandfather's office. Shouldn't the old man have returned to Chicago by now? After all, he'd turned the running of Sweet River Ranch over to Bryce's practically perfect older brother.

Ugh. This reminded Bryce way too much of summonses to the dean's office back in college. He'd been on probation more often than he cared to recall, but a Sullivan surname had its perks, and he hadn't been expelled.

He tapped on the office door. It stood slightly ajar, so he straightened his shoulders, pushed it open, and stepped inside.

Grandfather nodded from behind his desk. No smile creased his face. "Thank you for coming, Bryce."

Like he'd had a choice. When the person who held your purse strings called, you showed up with a salute. But at least the other desks in the room were unoccupied. Bless Grandfather for that small mercy. Bryce's brother and cousin didn't need to witness his dressing-down for whatever his most recent infraction proved to be.

Since when did he care about that? Huh.

"Good morning, Grandfather. What can I do for you today?"

"Have a seat."

Not a three-second meeting then. Bryce sat, keeping his back straight and trying to maintain eye contact, which proved more difficult than it ought to be. The old man's eyes pierced his like a hawk's focused on its prey.

No fidgeting. Just wait.

"I've had a job application from one Madison Woodrow."

Bryce forgot to breathe. He'd enjoyed every minute of evading Madison. Why else had he jumped on the chance to move to Montana when Grandfather summoned all his grandsons not quite two years back? That and staying on payroll, of course. Bryce wasn't stupid. He knew which side his bread was buttered on. Sullivan Enterprise's side.

"Oh?" He tried for a nonchalant question. Probably sounded more like an adolescent boy's squeak. He cleared his throat. "I thought Tate was handling all the personnel these days."

"Madison came directly to me."

Bryce shifted in the chair. "I didn't realize you were acquainted with her or her family."

Grandfather's shrug was all but imperceptible.

"It's January," Bryce said into the silence. "We don't have any openings until the tourist season picks up in spring."

The old man's bushy eyebrows rose. "There is always an opportunity for the right applicant. With our chef on her honeymoon, we have an immediate need in the kitchen. It's too much for Eryn on her own. Then, when Nadine and Keith return, Eryn will shift to the gift shop, and Madison can continue on. She is the perfect solution."

Was it just two days ago that Bryce's kid brother, Maxwell, had proposed to Eryn? And look how the tides were already turning. "The gift shop will hardly be a full-time job for Eryn until the tourists return."

Grandfather studied him for a long moment. "I have determined otherwise."

Of course, he had. Because he was as committed to rewarding his favorites, like Maxwell and Tate, as he was to punishing the least of them, like Bryce.

"Well, that's great, then. Thanks for giving me a heads-up." Bryce made to stand.

"Not so fast."

Bryce sank back onto the hard chair.

"Please inform me of the details of your relationship with Madison Woodrow."

"Didn't she already tell you?" She'd likely contacted the Sullivan patriarch with an entire sob story of how Bryce had disappeared from her life, but he could pin that on Grandfather. Well, not the ghosting so much. Just the move to Montana.

Elbows on his desk, Grandfather steepled his hands, his gaze never wavering. "I'd like to hear your side."

"We dated for several months. I tried to break up with her, but she kept showing up, rather clingy, as though I owed her something. Then you bought this ranch, I moved to Montana, and the rest is history." True, every word of it. Bryce had merely left out a few details.

Grandfather's scrutiny went on and on as though he could read Bryce's deepest thoughts. Could see the guilt and the regret that Bryce had locked way down deep. Everyone thought Bryce was a certain kind of guy? Fine. He'd prove them right. Wasn't that how life worked?

Well, not in everyone's world, apparently, but it made sense in Bryce's. Until it didn't.

A mouse being stared at by a hawk would doubtless have darted away by now, only to be grabbed by merciless talons. Bryce would not bolt. Would not break. He held Grandfather's gaze with all the strength he could muster. It was barely enough.

Finally, the old man's shoulders relaxed. "She's starting here today, working with Eryn while Nadine and Keith are away. I expect you to treat her with respect."

Bryce gave a sharp nod, not trusting his voice. Maxwell's girlfriend had been Aunt Nadine's kitchen helper for several months. She didn't have Nadine's years of experience cooking for a crowd — although not many workers remained at the ranch over the winter months — and Bryce could believe she needed help for the next two weeks. Maybe that's only how long Madison would be here. Maybe Bryce could avoid her. He could swing down to Jewel Lake this afternoon and pick up easy food to fix for himself in staff housing for a while.

Grandfather looked out the window, where snow fell softly. "There's quite a storm rolling in. It's good nearly everyone got away right after the wedding, because travel might be difficult for a while."

Scratch that trip to the Super One in town, then. But it might also mean Madison couldn't make it up the ranch road today. For the first time since Grandfather's summons, Bryce felt a flicker of hope. Maybe whatever Madison was up to would be foiled before it started. She was a city girl, through and through. She didn't belong on a ranch out west any more than Bryce did.

Although, it was kind of growing on him, and it wasn't entirely because of avoiding Madison, like it had been at first. He hadn't ridden horseback since summer camp way back in his childhood, but he'd enjoyed getting out on Kennedy nearly every week. Sure, there were riding stables near Chicago, but he'd never bothered. He'd been too busy living it up.

A tap sounded on the office door.

"Come in," Grandfather called, rising.

He'd been expecting... oh, no. Bryce sprang to his feet just as the woman entered the room.

Madison.

Her long red hair flowed over her shoulders, and her green eyes stared straight at him with no discernible expression. She looked just as good as she ever had. Her beauty had never been the problem.

Bryce moistened his lips. "Madison. What a surprise to see you here." Also, drat. She'd made it up the mountain before the storm. Now he'd be stuck with her.

Her chin rose slightly. "Bryce Sullivan. I am not surprised in the least to see you here."

Fair enough. He nodded. "Well, you caught up with me. Congratulations?"

"You don't know the half of it."

Nor did he wish to. On the other hand, there was also a lot she didn't know about him. Perhaps they were even.

"Please, have a seat." Grandfather waved toward the guest chairs then gave Bryce a sharp eye. "Both of you."

Hadn't Bryce been punished enough?

But the old man signed his paychecks, and no one else was going to offer Bryce a position that paid as well, especially if Grandfather put out the word that he was the family's black sheep.

Bryce resumed his seat as Madison took the one next to him.

She smelled of Carolina Herrera as she always had. The fragrance threatened to send Bryce down memory lane, but he'd be strong. He had to be.

MADISON PERCHED on the edge of the wooden guest chair. This had been a really, *really* bad idea, but she was out of options. Dad had been right about that.

Mr. Sullivan stood behind his desk, looking between her and Bryce. Finally, he nodded. "I'll leave you two to talk for a few minutes. I'm sure you have much to catch up on. When you're ready, Madison, I'll meet you in the dining hall. I'm sure Bryce will be happy to show you the way."

The only place Bryce would be happy to show her was likely to an unheated trappers cabin in the middle of the wilderness where she would freeze to death or be devoured by wolves.

"Certainly, sir," Bryce said.

Huh. Madison had finally found the one person Bryce spoke to respectfully. She should have contacted Mr.

Sullivan a long time ago. Or, possibly, she should have stayed away forever.

No. She needed to be here. Not for her own sake, but for Everly's.

How could it possibly be in her daughter's best interest to know her father? When Everly's father was self-centered, pampered Bryce Sullivan?

Dad and Nancy said it was. Said a girl needed her father, no matter what. Even if he were a criminal in prison? Madison had joked. Dad had said yes, even then.

For all his faults, at least Bryce wasn't that.

The door clicked closed behind Mr. Sullivan. The man must be over 80, but he had the bearing of a much younger man. He was obviously still on top of his game.

But now Madison was left in this awkward space with Bryce. The last time they'd been alone together — she shoved the memory out of her mind.

"Why, Madison?" Bryce surged to his feet and paced across the room before whirling to face her. "Why could you not leave well enough alone? Why track me down two full years after we broke up? What kind of compulsive, desperate woman does that?"

The kind who'd been left pregnant? But Madison tightened her lips. She'd tested assorted scenarios in her mind as to telling Bryce about his child, but she couldn't get the words out. What if, with all his family's money and influence, he decided to take Everly from her? She couldn't risk that. She had to get to know the guy Bryce was now to determine if he warranted the revelation.

He deserves to know, Madison.

Get out of my head, Dad.

She was here only because her father had pushed her. He called it encouragement, but it had been more than that. He'd refused to take no for an answer. At the first sign of Madison weakening, he'd booked a family ski vacation to Jewel Lake, complete with a suite rental. Madison's sister and brother-in-law and their two kids were also at the hotel. One big, happy, *pushy* family.

"I asked you a question, Madison."

Her chin came up as she faced Bryce. "It was time."

He growled. "A breakup is a breakup. People do it all the time, and the girl doesn't follow the guy to the ends of the earth two years later to get one last kick at the seat of his pants."

"This is the ends of the earth?"

"Compared to Chicago, it sure is. Seriously, Madison. We're over, and no amount of begging will change that. Say your piece and get back to the city where you belong."

Begging? Her ire ramped up along with her eyebrows. She could drop-kick Mr. Ego to the tile floor in two seconds flat, all without a single physical motion. But did Bryce really deserve to know the truth? Wasn't it better if he thought she was weird and obsessive than offering him the tool to ruin her life on a silver platter?

Dad said Bryce would never do that, but Madison wasn't so sure. What would stop him from using his family's money to keep Everly and send Madison packing?

He wouldn't do that.

But he might.

He glared at her through narrowed eyes, his jaw in a stubborn set.

What had she expected? That he'd claim how much he

missed her and, of course, he'd welcome the child he hadn't known existed, and they could float above all the troublesome issues as though they weren't real or didn't have the power to trip them up?

Okay, only one of the hundreds of scenarios had looked like that. Madison hadn't realized how much the hope in that one schema had taken hold in her heart.

It was now dashed. Completely, irrevocably dashed.

"I have my reasons," she said carefully.

He scoffed and whirled toward the window.

Behind him, large snowflakes drifted past in thick succession. Good thing she'd brought her bags with her, planning to stay for a few days before checking in with her family in Jewel Lake. Everly would be fine without her. Lacey would make sure of it. She'd been babysitting Everly on and off for over a year now. The little girl was practically like one of Lacey's own kids.

"This isn't where you belong, Madison. You and I both know it. Just let the past go. Please."

Madison rose. "No. Would you kindly show me to the dining hall?"

"Whatever," he muttered.

"And I'm pretty sure it's in this building, so don't get any ideas about taking me outside and losing me in this blizzard."

"Now there's a thought."

She stared at him. "That's beneath even you, Bryce."

"Even me? You have no idea what's beneath me. You and I never had that sort of relationship."

No, it had been 99% physical, and they sure hadn't

wasted the other 1% on delving deeply into what made each other tick. "That is sadly true."

He huffed then strode to the door, opened it, and gestured with a bow. "After you."

Madison gave it less than a week before she abandoned this dumb idea of letting Bryce in on her biggest secret. Surely even Dad would realize it was futile once she'd told him about Bryce's attitude.

Except he'd thought even a convicted criminal should know.

Whatever. She'd figure it out as she went along.

CHAPTER TWO

This is the dining hall." Bryce gestured before crossing his arms.

What would Madison have done without this gracious tour guide? "Thank you, Bryce." She shot him a nasty look before turning to look at the space and the commercial kitchen beyond the serving counter.

"That was quick," Mr. Sullivan observed, glancing between them. "Did you two clear the air?"

Was the old man senile? Of course, they hadn't cleared the air. Madison gave her head a slight shake. Surely, he would give her the space to reveal her secret in her own time. Surely, he realized how difficult Bryce could be.

A woman about her own age stood beside Mr. Sullivan, nervously twisting her hands together. Her long blond hair was tied back. Madison would need to do the same to work in a kitchen.

Seriously. A kitchen. Beggars couldn't be choosers, and she'd only committed to two weeks while the regular chef was away, though Mr. Sullivan had asked for more. She'd had to take a leave-of-absence from her medical transcriptionist position, and Raj had not been happy.

"This is Eryn Ralston," Mr. Sullivan announced. "She moved here from Kansas in October, and she's engaged to Bryce's brother Maxwell. She has quite a lot of cooking experience, but having help cooking for the winter crew will be very beneficial. Eryn, this is Madison Woodrow, a former... acquaintance of Bryce's."

Bryce snorted.

Madison felt like doing the same, but she had an impression to make. She smiled at the young woman and held out her hand. "I'm pleased to meet you, Eryn. I'm sure we'll get along great."

Bryce made a choking sound.

Juvenile. What had she ever seen in him? Right, she'd been just as committed to avoiding responsibility as he had back then. Pregnancy had a way of changing a person's priorities.

A fleeting smile crossed Eryn's face as she returned the handshake. "I'm really glad to have your help."

Honesty compelled Madison. "I don't have much cooking experience, but I'm good at following directions."

Eryn cast a panicked look at the old man, but he just smiled and patted her shoulder. "You two will be fine, Eryn. Nadine made sure everything was in order with menus and all before she left."

"Right. She did." Eryn's shoulders straightened. "When are you starting?"

"I'm not sure." Madison looked at Mr. Sullivan.

"Bryce will bring Madison's bags in. She'll have room

#206 in the lodge for the time being. If she's still here in April, we'll reevaluate her living space. So, let's give her a couple of hours to settle in while Bryce shows her around the ranch." He checked his watch and turned to Bryce. "Can you have Madison back here, ready to work, by 3:00?"

"I can have her back in five minutes."

The old man's bushy eyebrows peaked. "You can hardly give her a tour in that amount of time."

"It's snowing." Bryce pointed at the tall windows flanking the fireplace in the adjoining great room. "Quite heavily, I might add. Perhaps the tour can wait."

He wasn't wrong about the snow. Visibility had been minimal on her journey up the ranch road an hour ago, making driving the rented Jeep treacherous, though she'd had plenty of winter driving experience in Pennsylvania. But now she couldn't see much beyond the glass wall besides thick flakes.

There was more to see indoors. Leather loveseats and club chairs formed several groupings in the great room. A fire danced on the stone hearth, warming the space in both ambience and temperature.

She could be thankful she'd be allowed to sleep inside this building. Her research of Sweet River Ranch a few weeks ago had indicated staff housing in a cluster of duplexes a quarter mile from the main lodge.

Mr. Sullivan studied Bryce a moment before nodding. "Please assist Madison with her things. Kaci has freshened the room and left the door open."

"Yes, sir." Bryce's respectful response was at odds with the anger burning in his eyes when he turned to Madison.

"Or you could just toss me the keys and I'll get them myself. There's no point in both of us getting cold."

He meant that there was no point in spending a few minutes together. Madison was tempted to agree. Very tempted. But Dad had conspired with Mr. Sullivan, and she wasn't going to get away with avoiding Bryce here at the ranch. She had the benefit of knowing what was going on. Poor Bryce had been completely blindsided and still had no clue.

Don't start feeling sorry for the reprobate.

Madison braced herself as she fingered the key fob in her pocket. "I'll give you a hand, but I appreciate the help. Thanks."

"Don't trust me with your riches?" His tone mocked as he strode to the entry area then plucked a down parka from a hook.

He had no idea how true that was. "You hit the nail on the head. The Jeep is just outside."

"Jeep? That's not much of a Chicago vehicle."

"I flew out, so this is a rental."

He rolled his eyes. "Of course. Lead the way."

She slipped into her own coat and opened the outside door. Wind blasted past, blowing the snow nearly horizontally. The white Jeep was all but invisible although only 10 or 15 feet away. Madison tipped her collar up and double-clicked the fob. The lights flashed as it unlocked. She hurried over — brr — and opened the hatch.

Bryce was right there to pull out the two biggest suitcases. "You have a lot of luggage for someone staying two weeks."

"Two weeks minimum. Didn't your grandfather tell you

I might be staying longer to help in the kitchen?" Unless she turned tail and ran, the most likely scenario.

"I didn't believe him. Still don't. You're not made for rural life, Madison. You're too much of a princess to fit in here. Just accept it and go back home. No need to unpack."

"I suppose you enjoy being a cowboy?" she challenged.

"Shows how little you know me," he shot back, already back on the lodge steps with his load.

Madison grabbed her backpack and two smaller bags. That only left a couple for Bryce's return trip. She pulled the hatch closed — no sense allowing the vehicle to fill with snow — and followed him back into the lodge. She toed off her boots where he did then trailed him up a wide staircase.

Didn't they have elevators in this place? Although he had the heavier load by far, Bryce wasn't complaining, so she wouldn't, either.

She followed him into Room #206. This was more like it. The king bed lay draped in luscious-looking bedding, while the furniture was a rustic yet elegant pine. A matching lowboy with a large mirror looked to have enough space for her things in conjunction with the walk-in closet.

Madison took a few steps into the room so she could check out the adjoining marble bathroom. Luxury, indeed. The staff housing images online lacked all of this grace and beauty.

Thanks, Mr. Sullivan. Whatever she'd done to deserve this step up, she was grateful.

Bryce had set down the two suitcases and was disappearing out the door by the time she turned toward him.

He'd be back momentarily with the rest of her belongings. The Jeep contained zero evidence she had a child. No carseat, no diaper bag, no basket overflowing with toys. Everything was with her family at the hotel in Jewel Lake.

Tears pricked Madison's eyes. How was she ever going to endure this separation from her daughter? Everly was only 15 months old, too young for explanations. She had her cousins to play with at the hotel, her auntie and uncle, her grandparents. But surely, she would miss her mama as much as her mama would miss her.

The fastest way to reunification would be to break the news to Bryce as soon as he walked back into the room. Then Madison could hightail it back down the mountain and off to someplace far, far away. Ugh, not until the snow cleared.

Although the revelation was more likely to result in him exercising his paternal rights over Everly to spite Madison.

Madison couldn't take the risk. Not yet.

BRYCE PARKED the last of Madison's things in her room. "How did you score a room in the lodge? None of the staff lives in here." He leaned against the doorway to the walk-in closet where she hung her clothes.

She backed deeper into the space, eyes wide.

Great, now he was scaring her. He only meant to prod her to leave the ranch, not to make her fear for her life or virtue. He'd already taken her virtue, and he had no desire to revisit that scenario.

Well, yes, Madison was just as beautiful as she'd been back then. Her red hair was natural, she'd assured him, not out of a bottle. Her figure was maybe a little rounder than it had been, but that wasn't a negative.

Not that he noticed.

He. Did. Not. Care.

Best to focus on all the things he hadn't liked about her, which was mostly how possessive she'd become almost immediately. That exclusivity had been fun for like a week before Bryce felt the claustrophobia of the walls leaning in around him. After that, the more he'd tried to gain distance from her, the more she'd been in his face like a headlock he couldn't remove.

When he was a teen, he'd scoffed at his mother's admonitions about casual sex. She'd said there wasn't anything casual about it, that each encounter set permanent hooks in both partners' hearts, whether intended or not.

Bryce believed her now. Everyone thought he'd continued his irresponsible ways here in Montana, and he let them believe what they wanted. Yeah, he'd flirted constantly and dated a lot, but Madison had taught him one major lesson, and that was not to let more of those hooks grab into his flesh. A night of passion wasn't worth the aftermath.

He blinked.

She still stared at him, a hanger in one hand, a green dress that matched her eyes in the other. Poised, waiting for whatever he was going to say or do.

All the bravado wafted out of him. Those hooks Mom spoke of had been deeper than he thought. "Why, Madison?"

She pivoted, hung the dress, and reached for another.

Why so many? None of the women here wore dresses, except occasionally to church. It was a ranch, for goodness' sake. Sure, it was mostly for tourists, but it was the West. Just went to show how little she knew about Montana.

"You came a long way to not talk to me."

"I told you, it was time."

Bryce reined in his temper, picturing Kennedy rearing back, front hooves cleaving the air. He'd kept his seat on the big bay, and he'd keep it now. "Did you only just figure out where I was? I didn't think there was much of a secret to it."

Come to think of it, she'd left Chicago, too, if mutual friends were to be believed. After he'd moved to Montana, she'd gone to her dad's place in Pittsburgh. Bryce's informant had laughed and said Madison's mom had been furious with her for running off to Daddy.

Wonder why?

But it didn't matter nearly as much as why she was here now. What did 'it was time' mean? Two years had gone by. For all he cared, another 10 or 50 would have been just fine.

"I wanted a change of pace," Madison said finally.

Bryce stared at her, trying to remember the question.

"And I wondered what had drawn you to Montana. So, here I am."

"That's the best you can come up with? I broke up with you, Madison. I called us off in mid-January. It's been two solid years. And now you are curious about why I live in Montana?" He crossed his arms and shook his head. "I'm not buying what you're selling."

"You don't have to believe me for it to be true."

He rolled his eyes. "Come on, Madison. Try again."

Her chin lifted. "I became a Christian last year. The Bible tells me to forgive those who've wronged me."

"Forgive me from a distance. I'm happy to haul your stuff back to the Jeep and wave goodbye."

"There's a blizzard."

"You sure picked your timing, didn't you?"

Madison glared at him. "The snowstorm wasn't in the forecast when I booked my flight."

Quite premeditated, then. "When did you ask my grandfather for a job?"

"In Chicago the week before Christmas."

"May I ask it again? Why?" Bryce let his frustration out as he growled the final word.

Madison flinched. "I believe I answered that question."

"Not to my satisfaction."

"I'm not here to satisfy you."

If daggers could have shot out of her piercing eyes, Bryce would have been pinned to the wall. Possibly dead. Certainly bleeding.

"And you can take that any which way you want. I mean all of them. I'm not here to please you."

"You have achieved your objective of not pleasing me."

She licked her finger and chalked one up on an invisible tally board. "One point for me."

"Sheesh, Madison. Are we going to play childish games?" He'd vastly preferred the more adult kind, but not anymore. All he wanted was for her to disappear and leave him in peace.

"Are you a Christian, Bryce?"

"What business is it of yours?"

"Are you?"

"Of course, I am. A guy can't be a Sullivan in good standing without showing up at church every Sunday morning."

"That doesn't make you a Christian any more than..." She waved a hand. "Standing in a stable makes you a horse."

"Oh, look at you trying to sound like a western woman."

Madison bit her lip. "I only want you to know God's peace and forgiveness like I have."

Yeah, well, that wasn't the sort of God Bryce knew. When the Almighty looked at Bryce, it was with woeful eyes. Disappointed eyes. Judgy eyes.

"Great for you." Bryce shoved away from the doorway. "Have fun settling into your fancy abode and slaving your fingers to a bone in the kitchen. And do us both a favor and head back to the city the minute the snowstorm ends. You're not needed here, Madison. Go home."

CHAPTER THREE

She couldn't put off going downstairs much longer. Her clothes and toiletries were settled into their temporary homes. Everly's spare stuffed rabbit leaned against the pillows — the toddler had identical ones for home and for Lacey's house, so she wouldn't miss this version of Bunny. Madison changed the wallpaper on her phone's lockscreen lest someone pick it up when she wasn't looking. It had a passcode — Everly's birthday — so no one could swipe through her photos, but the lockscreen would be visible to anyone who touched the device.

Her tablet with her favorite photo of the two of them as wallpaper was in the nightstand drawer. No one would be snooping in her bedroom.

They'd better not be, anyway.

Bryce would never stoop that low. He had no clue about the real reason Madison was at Sweet River Ranch. He thought she was being petty.

Little did he know.

Tell him, Madison.

Get out of my head, Dad.

Seemed like Allen Woodrow didn't need to be present for him to keep pushing his agenda. Well, she was here at the ranch, wasn't she? She'd seen Bryce and was biding her time. He hadn't earned the right to knowledge.

Madison paused in her luxurious private bath for prayers for wisdom. For patience. For love.

Heavens, not romantic love for Bryce. Just that the love of Christ would shine through her. That she'd be a mature, kind, helpful person everyone at the ranch would appreciate being around.

The kind of woman Bryce Sullivan would regret snubbing.

Again, no.

No wonder she hadn't made an effort to contact Bryce since the initial efforts when she'd discovered her pregnancy. He brought out such a jumble of emotions that she couldn't keep on top of. She definitely needed the Lord's help.

She tucked her phone into her hip pocket, twisted her hair into a quick French knot, and practiced her smile in the large mirror.

Here we go, God. Help me, please.

Madison descended the staircase, crossed the great room, and entered the dining hall. Neither Bryce nor the rest of the ranch residents were around, other than the young woman in the kitchen.

Eryn was about to become Madison's best friend. She could only hope the other woman was up for it, but if they were to work together for two weeks, they'd need to get along really well.

"Hi, Eryn! It's 3:00, and I'm reporting for duty. What would you like me to do?" Madison crossed to the smallest of the three sinks to wash her hands.

"Hi. Maybe you can chop some onions and celery and mushrooms for the chili? I'm just starting to brown the ground beef. After that, maybe you could fix a salad."

"Sure." Thanks to her stepmom's coaching in the past year, Madison had a clue how to chop those things. Maybe she could do this.

Eryn pulled celery and mushrooms from the fridge and pointed out the magnetic knife holder on the wall above the built-in cutting board. "I'm only in charge here temporarily. This is Nadine's domain, but she's on her honeymoon."

Madison began to peel an onion from the basket on the counter. "Tell me about Nadine."

"Oh! She's Mr. Sullivan's daughter, and he only discovered her existence about two years ago. Can you just imagine the shock of discovering he had a daughter in her mid-fifties?"

Yep. Madison had no trouble imagining that. In her perfect world, Bryce wouldn't find out until he was an old man, either, not that she was going to divulge her secret to someone she'd just met. "That's crazy. How did it happen?"

"He'd had an affair with his secretary—"

"I meant, how did he find out?" Maybe she could get some tips.

"Nadine's mother, Eleanor, refused to tell her who her father was, though she asked many times. But then she found her entire family through one of those genealogy sites that links people's DNA results, and she went to Chicago to confront her father."

So that's why Mr. Sullivan knew how to check Everly's DNA back in December and ascertain that Madison told the truth about the toddler's paternity. Not many people of his generation had a clue how to do much of anything online, but he hadn't hesitated.

Madison could hardly fault him for wanting proof before falling in with Dad's scheme to push her and Bryce together for the revelation. Dad and Nancy weren't exactly paupers, but they weren't in the same league as Bryce's family.

"Nadine said she felt like part of her was always missing. Everyone else had dads, but not her, even though her mom married, and she had two younger half-brothers. She knew her mother's husband wasn't really her father, and she wanted to know where she came from. She resented her mom for not telling her the one thing she most wanted to know."

Ugh. Could Madison change the subject already? She didn't want to think about Everly's future questions. It was bad enough dealing with her own turmoil in the moment. Had Nadine's mom struggled like Madison did? She must have, but she'd stood her ground. Why?

"Nadine married my father on New Year's Eve," Eryn went on.

"Wait, what?" Madison had missed a transition in there somewhere.

Eryn pivoted from the stove to look at her from wide eyes. "I… what did you miss? I said Mr. Sullivan bought this ranch to integrate his daughter and his two newfound grandsons into the family. Nadine's husband had passed away, and my mom died—" Eryn gulped "—when I was 12. Dad and Nadine hit it off when we moved here."

How had Madison blanked out for so long? Eryn must think Madison found her story boring. Far from it.

"I hope you're happy with her for a stepmom!"

"She's lovely. You'll enjoy working with her in the kitchen when she returns."

If Madison stuck it out that long. But she would definitely like to hear Nadine's story from the woman herself... and also Eleanor's. Would anyone think her obsession strange? Only if she let it show. She'd be careful. Everly's entire future depended on her mama's every word.

"I'm sure I'll like her. How did you and your dad come to move here? Mr. Sullivan said you'd come from Kansas recently?"

Eryn's cheeks pinked. "It's a long story."

Madison bent over the cutting board. "We have a lot of time while we cook."

"I HAVEN'T SEEN a storm this bad in a long time." Maxwell stomped the snow off his boots before removing them.

"Probably been 10, 12 years for this part of Montana." Weston hung his down parka.

Bryce waited his turn to shed his outerwear. "It sure feels nice in here with that fire going. The heater in the duplex is struggling to keep the frost out."

Weston looked thoughtful. "The snow is heavy on the

power lines. I should check the fuel in the generators. We'll likely need them."

"Aren't all the gas cans in the fuel shed full?" Maxwell wanted to know.

"Unless someone has used them that I don't know of. I'll need fuel for the ATV and snowmobiles for feeding." Weston shook his head. "Darrel and I might also need help hauling hay."

"I can help with that," Bryce put in. "I've got nothing better to do." It would beat sitting around the lodge near Madison, and it wasn't like there was any landscaping to be done in the dead of winter.

Maxwell pivoted and stared at Bryce as though he'd grown horns.

"What? I can be helpful."

"Sure. Okay. Good."

Bryce narrowed his gaze. "Shut it."

His brother snorted a laugh as he turned away. "Gotta go see my girl."

Must be nice. Although Madison was probably in the kitchen with Eryn. Did Bryce want her back? Not after trying to rid himself of her memory for two years, no.

But somebody. No one currently living at Sweet River. Not Kaci or Janessa or any of the other single women. Maybe there would be a new hire come spring with whom he'd hit it off.

Being alone was getting old.

He was getting old. Thirty was in the rearview mirror.

Did that mean he was ready to settle down? His brothers made it look attractive, as did his cousins. But for Bryce?

Madison was right here. She wouldn't have sought him out if she didn't feel anything for him at all, right?

She was too clingy.

Was *Eryn* too clingy? Not according to his brother. Maxwell reveled in being Eryn's sunrise and sunset.

How about Stephanie, Bryce's older brother's wife? She'd sure been focused on nailing Tate down a couple of years ago, and Tate had been all in.

Maybe the fault wasn't with Madison. Maybe it was with Bryce.

No. He'd broken things off, and she hadn't let him go. It was on her.

More voices and laughter, more stomping boots sounded on the deck just outside the door, as Bryce followed Maxwell and Tate toward the delectable fragrances coming from the kitchen around the corner.

Didn't smell like Madison had burned anything. Not like that time she'd scorched the fried eggs in Bryce's condo. He'd ended up tossing the pan as well as the contents. It had been his favorite pan, too.

Maybe she'd learned some cooking skills in the past couple of years. Bryce couldn't even begin to count how many ways his own horizons had broadened since moving to the ranch.

"Mmm, chili." Maxwell stood behind Eryn with his arms wrapped around her as he nuzzled her neck.

Ugh. Bryce didn't need to watch their PDA.

Madison turned his way.

He didn't need to watch her, either. He pivoted to say something to his cousin, but Weston was kissing his fiancée.

Love — mushiness — was everywhere he turned.

Kaci had entered the space along with a few others. She tolerated Bryce at best, so he wasn't about to insert himself into her conversation so Madison could observe Kaci snubbing him.

Was this really what his life had come to? Realizing he didn't have a single friend who wanted to hang out with him? His brothers and cousins sort of had to put up with him, but that wasn't the same thing as an actual friendship.

What about the crowd he'd hung out with in Chicago? They'd mostly been there for the booze and the parties. Even Drew had only checked in with Bryce once or twice, the last time over a year ago.

Bryce was absolutely, undeniably, pathetically alone.

"Good afternoon, Bryce."

He turned to see Grandfather's former lover. "Hi, Eleanor. I didn't realize you'd stayed up at the ranch after the wedding."

"Walter asked me to, since he planned to stay in Montana for a couple of weeks." She looked down. "He requested the opportunity to spend some time together without Nadine."

Bryce grimaced. That just solidified his realization of his own loneliness. Even his 82-year-old grandfather had more moves, more of a social life, than he did. More prospects. Was there any chance this pair would marry?

Bryce couldn't imagine a wedding like that, mostly because he didn't want to think of what came after. Ugh. Not going there.

He gestured toward the windows, where the sky was

completely dark save for snow blasting past, glowing in the porch lights. "You may not get out any time soon."

"It does look like quite a storm," Eleanor agreed. "But I've weathered some big ones in my life."

Were they still talking about snow? "I'm sure you have."

"Walter assures me the lodge is set up to stay warm and lit no matter what."

"He's assured me of the same thing. We may find out if he's right."

Eleanor nodded. "It's entirely likely. The lines are already drooping from the weight of all that thick, wet snow. It would take a miracle to sustain power."

Bryce glanced at the window again and shifted uneasily. It was one thing to spout bravado beforehand, but it was another thing entirely to endure any sort of hardship. Guys like him didn't *do* hardship.

"Is everyone here?" Grandfather stepped up beside Eleanor and looked around.

"I think so." Not that the old man was asking Bryce, precisely.

"Then let us pray. Father God, we thank You for a warm, safe building to weather this storm. You are always our shelter in times of need. Thank You for this delicious food and the hands that have prepared it. Please bless it so that we may honor you with health and strength in our bodies. In Jesus' name, amen."

At least Grandfather's grace was usually short and sweet.

The group began to form a line while Eryn and Madison served up chili, cornbread, and salad.

Bryce found himself near the end with only Grandfather and Eleanor behind him. He grabbed a tray when it was his turn and accepted the bowl of chili Eryn passed him. "Thank you." Then he had to be equally polite to Madison. Grandfather wasn't beyond giving him a swift kick in the rear if he felt it was warranted. It might put his back out, but it wouldn't stop him, and then Bryce would feel guilty.

He hated feeling guilty.

But it seemed he was doomed to it.

CHAPTER FOUR

Two mornings later, Madison awoke to absolute stillness and silence, quite a shock from the howling wind that had formed a constant soundtrack since her arrival.

She burrowed deeper under the down comforter. The murky light from the windows indicated it was too early to rise and shine... but what time was it, really? She twisted on her pillow to see her bedside clock, but it was blank.

Blank?

Madison surged to sitting and reached for her phone. A generic photo of the Chicago waterfront lay behind the time. 7:40.

No way! They were to serve breakfast at eight! She flung the cover off and rushed into her bathroom. There was no time for a shower, so she scrubbed her face with water, brushed her teeth and hair, and donned jeans and a sweatshirt before hurrying toward the staircase.

The fireplace was lit, and Mr. Sullivan, Eleanor, and

several others chatted in the leather seating. A clank of pans came from the kitchen.

Madison's face burned. She was the only one who'd overslept, and she had the least excuse. It was nearly 10 in the Eastern time zone. She hadn't slept this late since well before Everly's birth.

Eryn glanced up at Madison's entry to the kitchen.

"I'm sorry. With the power out, my alarm didn't go off."

"No worries. The guys and Paisley have taken the snowmobiles out to feed the cows and horses, and they won't be back for a while. Everyone slept a bit late."

"Okay. What would you like me to do? Also, how does the kitchen have electricity?" Not that it was quite as well-lit as usual.

"Generators. We do need to conserve, as there is a finite amount of fuel to run them and other necessities. So, I plan to bake an oven full of pans of frittata this morning to limit the amount of energy use. We can have the leftovers tomorrow. Ready to chop?"

"Sure." Madison knew her way around the kitchen by now. She and Eryn prepped the pans then popped them in the oven. "What happens now? How long will the power be off?"

Eryn shook her head. "I have no idea. It's my first winter here, and the first time the lines have been down. I imagine the surrounding area will be suffering the same fate, and I don't know how far up or down the restoration list Sweet River is."

Now that Madison wasn't busy, agitation threatened to turn to panic. Did the lakefront hotel have generators? Was her family okay? How about Everly? She tried to push the thoughts away. There wasn't anything she could do to help them. It couldn't possibly take long to restore the lines. Maybe a few hours. A day or two at the most.

Mr. Sullivan stood across the serving counter. "Everyone needs to move into the lodge for the duration. I should have made that call at the first sign this storm was bigger than most. As soon as all the animals and people have been fed, we'll get everyone to gather their necessities while Weston and Maxwell drain the duplexes' waterlines. At least it's not crazy cold yet to add freezing pipes to our concerns."

That meant Bryce would be in her space all day. She could only be thankful he was on the livestock crew. That would occupy a few of his hours a day.

"How long do you think this will last?" Eryn sounded nervous.

The old man shook his head. "There's no way to know, but we need to prepare as though it will be a week or two."

Madison gaped. "A week? *Or two?*"

"I'm sure it won't be that long, but I can't guarantee it… or anything at all. It only makes sense to conserve just in case."

Eryn twisted her hands together. "Are we camping out in the great room?"

Madison opened her mouth to invite Eryn to share her space, but Mr. Sullivan spoke first. "No. That's fine for an occasional party, but there are plenty of guest rooms on the second and third floors. It will give housekeeping something to do when normal life returns."

Kaci laughed as she crossed the dining hall. "Right, because it's so boring otherwise. It's a good idea, though.

It's not like we'll have a sudden influx of guests in this weather, so we might as well make use of the space and get comfortable."

"How are we heated?" Madison asked. She'd never wondered such things before. Bryce was right. She didn't belong in a mountain lodge far from home, but it wasn't like she could escape right now.

Or until she'd come clean. Ugh.

"We have a large propane tank to back-up wood and electric heat, and it was topped up in November. We can last the storm in here. It's the smaller buildings that have no backup." Grinning, Mr. Sullivan brushed his hands together.

The elderly man looked like he was quite enjoying this bit of adventure.

That made one of them. Although with Kaci, possibly two.

Madison did not appreciate trials. She liked her life neat, orderly, and predictable... at least, since Bryce had whirled in and then out of it. God seemed to have a sense of humor, and it was a different variety than humankind's. Was this God's way of shoving her and Bryce together so she'd have to spill the beans?

Not funny, God. I need more time.

Like He cared.

No, He did. He had saved her from her aimless, carnal life. She might have thought she'd made the choice to flee to Dad's house in Pittsburgh after discovering her pregnancy and being snubbed by Bryce, but God had led even that decision. He'd drawn her to Himself.

Had He let her down since then?

No, He had not. There was no need to panic. Madison could trust Him now, both for herself and for Everly.

"I'll post room assignments on the whiteboard," Kaci said.

"Hello, the house!" a male voice bellowed. "Are we welcome here?"

"Tate! Come in, boy. Have you got your family with you?"

"Sure do!" The man's voice lowered. "Here, Simon, let me get that zipper. Jamie! Boots on the mat, remember?"

The last remaining Sullivan brother, whom Madison hadn't met. The CEO of Sweet River Ranch now, he hadn't been in Chicago when she'd dated Bryce. Had he been in Kansas? Kansas sounded right.

Here she stood without a shower or a stitch of makeup. What kind of first impression was she making to the CEO? Out of her control. Everything had spun out of her control.

BRYCE MANAGED to avoid Madison for the next few hours. After working up a sweat feeding the cattle, he'd moved his toiletries and some clothes into the lodge, then helped Maxwell and Weston shut down the staff duplexes as they were vacated. Thankfully, the guest cabins had been winterized after Thanksgiving, so nothing would freeze in them.

But now the entire group had gathered again, waiting for their dinner summons. He wouldn't be able to retreat to his own turf — the room upstairs hardly counted, since it didn't even have light, let alone a working plug for his laptop. And his phone battery was rapidly draining, since service was intermittent, and the device was constantly searching for signal.

"Do we have a phone charging solution?" he asked Tate, who'd brought Stephanie and the boys to the lodge while he'd been out earlier. "I know there's no wi-fi, but the towers are still transmitting."

"Cadence thought of that. There's a USB power bar on the counter by the door." Tate pointed to the check-in desk. "We can use it when the generator is running, which will be for a couple of hours across mealtimes."

Bryce's eyebrows tipped up. "So little?"

"Just enough to keep the fridges and freezers doing their job. We can make do with everything else."

Easy for Tate to say. Still, they had no idea how long they'd be stranded here, or how long the fuel supply would need to hold out. They'd used a fair bit in the snowmobiles to feed the livestock, as well.

"Question for you." Tate lowered his voice and touched Bryce's arm.

"Yeah?" Bryce pulled away from his brother's touch.

"We'll get through tomorrow fine, but if we're still stuck the next day, would you be willing to take a snowmobile and sled down into town and get us more fuel? And maybe make sure the highways department and power company know we need help. We did leave a message but haven't heard back."

"Do they cover our ranch road?"

"Part of it, because there's public access to the river just a couple of miles down."

"Right. I forgot about that." Maybe he hadn't even

known. Why would he have cared? "So, will we use the tractor or the skid steer to plow that far?"

Tate chewed on his lip. "I hadn't thought of the skid steer, but it might be the better option. I'll talk to Weston about that. He's been tied up today with winterizing the duplexes, but he'll get on that tomorrow. With Keith away, he's got the most tractor experience, but you've probably driven the skid more. What do you say? Trip to Jewel Lake if needed?"

"Sure. Why not?" Bryce was likely the most dispensable member of the group, not that his brother was exactly risking his life. Hadn't he been looking for an excuse to get off the property? Here was one on a golden platter. More like a platter of solid ice, but still.

"I'll send someone with you to pick up kitchen supplies. Maybe Madison."

Bryce lowered his chin and glared at his brother. "Aren't you the funny one?"

"What? Why?" And Tate looked so innocent, too.

"It's enough — more than enough — that Grandfather hired her. Don't get in on forcing us together. We were over two years ago, and she's some sort of obsessive to have followed me here."

"She's the best one to go, though. Eryn... well, I don't think Maxwell would let me send her, even if he were the driver. She gets anxious so easily, but Madison seems like she'd be up for anything."

Oh, she definitely was, and it wasn't to her credit. Nor was it to his.

There, guilt. Take that. Bryce could admit to being at fault, at least partially.

"As I understand it, the menu and food Nadine left for these two weeks isn't necessarily the most power-saving." Tate waved a hand. "Or, maybe the power will be back by Thursday, and the trip will be moot."

"I sure hope so." Bryce pivoted on his heel. The generators were running right now, so he might as well get his phone charged. Just needed a cord from his room.

He came back down a moment later to find Grandfather and Eleanor facing each other over a cribbage board by the window. After plugging in his device, he pulled up a chair. "Who's winning?"

"She is." Grandfather groaned. "Beginner's luck."

"Beginner?" Eleanor raised her eyebrows. "You only assumed that. It's been a while, I'll grant you, but Randy and I played many a hand of crib."

Grandfather counted out his hand and moved his peg. "Tell me more about Randy."

Bryce shouldn't be eavesdropping. "I wonder what other games there are." They'd need something to occupy the long evening besides random chitchat. He'd read a book before it came to baring his soul, at least if there was some decent fiction in that shelving unit over there. He'd never checked. Weston and Graham were readers. Wasn't that enough for one family?

He opened the cupboard and found a few he remembered from his childhood — Monopoly, Clue, Risk — and a bunch he hadn't seen before. They could while away a few hours with that collection, if others were willing.

Look at him. Bryce Sullivan, team player.

Well, there was a first for everything.

"Whatcha doing, Unca Bryce?" Jamie tugged on his hand.

Bryce looked down at his nephew, his oldest brother's child. "Hey, kid. I was just looking for games to play."

The irony wasn't lost. He usually invented his own. Just not played with cards or boards.

Jamie peered at the cupboard. "Is there ones for kids?"

Wasn't he too young for even 'Go Fish'? Bryce doubted the boy recognized all his numbers yet. "I'm sure we can find something." What? No clue, but he could ask Stephanie or Tate for ideas.

"Yay! Thanks, Unca Bryce!" Jamie swung his hand, beaming up at him.

"You're pretty all right, kid." Bryce scrubbed his curly blond hair. "Did you know that?"

"Mama says my awesome."

"You are." But Stephanie wasn't Jamie's mom any more than Tate was his dad. The little boy had no memories of his parents. They'd died in a helicopter crash just after Jamie's first birthday, and good old Uncle Tate had stepped in. Then Stephanie had. And now they had another kid, who was not even a year old.

How time flew. Bryce hadn't seen much of Wally the last few years before the fatal accident. They hadn't seen eye-to-eye on much of anything. Big surprise there, with Wally all conscientious, working his way up in Sullivan Enterprises. If he'd still been alive, he'd be CEO here, not Tate. He, not Tate, would be raising Jamie.

Their mother wouldn't have suffered the rounds of depression she'd struggled with since her favorite son's death. Tate had taken over there, too.

Bryce should hate Tate, but it was impossible. The guy was too nice, too good at everything he did.

"Play cars wi' me?" Jamie towed Bryce toward the fireplace, where Simon had dumped all the contents from the toybox and climbed inside it himself.

"Sure. Why not?" Bryce lowered himself to the rug. "Which car can I play with?"

"Dis one. Is red."

Bryce buzzed the car around his knees while his nephew kept up a monologue with the other vehicles. But something was off. He felt the hair on the back of his neck prickling and glanced up.

Madison stood just inside the dining hall, staring at him with an indecipherable expression on her face.

What had he done wrong this time?

CHAPTER FIVE

Whew. At least she'd remembered to change her phone's background photo. Madison had never dreamed she'd be charging her device along with others in a long row. Even so, her case stood out with its colorful, dancing music-note background. She'd loved that it was different and showed several of her interests. Now, she wished she'd gone for a plain gray or something else invisible.

But her lifeline to Lacey and Everly was down to 6% power... not that she could get to Jewel Lake, even in case of an emergency. Madison snagged the last USB portal and laid her phone face down in case Lacey texted photos or something. Her phone definitely shouldn't fall into the wrong hands.

That one must be Bryce's with its cartoon guy in a suit, dancing. If she could pick his out of a lineup, he could likely do the same with hers. No matter. It needed charging, and she needed to be in the kitchen helping Eryn. The other woman was majorly stressed about conserving power while feeding a couple of dozen people.

Madison had never thought she was particularly good in emergencies, but she didn't panic like Eryn did. On the other hand, she wasn't responsible for all this. She was just a helper.

"If you place the pans this way, they'll all fit." Eleanor crouched in front of the oven, moving things around. "See?"

"Right. That makes sense. I wish we had thought to bake bread ahead."

"You're doing fine, dearie. You could conscript a few more helpers, you know. That young buck of yours could knead by hand if you showed him how."

Maxwell flexed his biceps as he grinned. "Sure could. At least, I think I could. I've never tried. Someone would have to show me."

"I don't know how to do it by hand, either." Eryn wrung her hands. "Nadine showed me with the machine, and that's what we've always done."

Eleanor shook her head. "Kids these days. Let me know when you want to start the next batch, and I'll teach whoever is willing to learn. I'd say not to bother with bread, but it's filling, and we need that right now."

"Okay. Thanks." Eryn's gaze fell on Madison standing nearby. "Have you ever kneaded bread without a machine?"

"Me?" Madison pressed her hand to her chest. Hadn't Eryn noticed how much she bumbled in the kitchen? She barely knew how to chop an onion. "Um, no."

Eryn took a few grounding breaths. "Okay. So that's all

the pans full of meatloaves and the other rack full of baking potatoes. I sure hope we have enough propane to last the storm."

Madison was no expert, but wasn't propane the least of their worries? From what she'd gathered, the cooking appliances used that fuel year 'round. The power outage wasn't causing them to cook more than usual, was it? And from what she'd figured out, the fuel that was at a premium for the generators and snowmobiles was a different kind altogether. But what did she know?

"It will be fine, dearie." Eleanor clapped her hands together. "Dinner is in the oven, everyone. Why don't we play something while it cooks?"

Madison blinked. The woman must be in her mid-70s. She'd probably weathered a storm or two in the past.

"Great idea!" Paisley sashayed in from the great room. "Charades it is."

A collective groan went up from everyone present.

"Oh, come on. You guys know you enjoyed it at Maxwell's birthday party in November."

"We recall no such thing," Maxwell quipped.

"Pictionary, then. It's one or the other for a group this size."

Madison was a better artist than actor. "Pictionary sounds good."

"I knew I liked you!" Paisley beamed at her. "Come on, everyone. Gather round, guys against girls. Weston, let's grab a couple of white-board easels and a bunch of markers. Come on!"

Weston shook his head, but he was grinning as he followed his fiancée toward the storage rooms.

One thing Madison hadn't counted on in coming here was all the romance. There were two newlywed couples — did Tate and Stephanie count, as they already had a baby? — and two engaged couples. It seemed hearts and kisses danced in the atmosphere.

She did *not* need the reminder that she and Bryce were done... except for their child. So, they weren't done, but they also weren't about to join the blissful couples. Or... maybe?

Tell him, sunshine.

Get out of my head, Dad.

The correct answer was no. She and Bryce weren't getting back together... but wouldn't that be best for Everly? Even if Bryce played nice, he'd want Madison to share. She'd seen him on the floor driving cars with his nephew, who was only a year older than their own daughter. He'd been surprisingly sweet with Jamie.

He would be that good with Everly.

How could she send a toddler back and forth between Pennsylvania and Montana? Maybe Bryce would move to Pittsburgh. No, she couldn't see it. He'd seemed to fit the Chicago scene so well, but Sweet River Ranch brought out a side of him she'd never dreamed existed.

Knowing he was a father would give him one more facet.

Motherhood had certainly changed everything for Madison. Was it only because their baby had grown inside her, creating a distinct bond? Or would Bryce feel a bond with Everly, too?

You should tell him, Madison.

Not right now, Dad. Shush.

But Dad's voice was getting more and more insistent as Madison became acquainted with the new Bryce, who seemed to be a nicer guy than she recalled. Had he changed in the past two years? She certainly had, so was it too much to expect he might have, as well?

It didn't say much for her taste in men that she'd fallen for the previous version of Bryce. She didn't need to go falling for the current version all over again. She'd become a Christian in the meanwhile, and didn't God say not to be unequally yoked with unbelievers? Bryce went to church and seemed to think that was all he needed. She knew better. She suspected he knew it, too.

"Ready?" Paisley set up a white-board while Weston dragged a second one into position a few feet away. "Bryce, want to get the game out of the cupboard?"

He rolled his eyes and shook his head, but still moved in that direction.

Bryce might wish to project a certain persona, but underneath, he was a decent guy.

And Madison really, really didn't want that to be the case. It made everything so much harder.

Don't even start with me, Dad.

Pictionary was just as dumb as charades. When Bryce had been thinking of group activities, he'd been thinking more of dominating the world in Risk than making verbal guesses for everyone to hear and judge.

At least, he was judging everyone else's contributions, trying to read extra into each shout-out, so weren't they doing the same to him? Maybe that was unique to him. After all, he wasn't really like anyone else. Not like his brothers, for sure. Not like anyone else here.

They were all avowed Jesus-followers, and Bryce didn't have the bandwidth to figure that out. He had no need for a crutch. He was doing fine on his own.

Well, sort of fine.

An all-play card was pulled when it was Madison's turn. Over here, Tate was drawing for the guys. Good. That meant Bryce could watch Madison for clues, and no one would think it was weird.

Not that he cared what others thought... wait. Hadn't he just admitted he did? Thankfully, that was just in his own head, and no one else was privy to that admission. They'd take it and run. Hold it over his head.

Madison stared at the card in her hand as she bit her lip and cast a frantic look his direction.

He managed to keep the snort inside. He was the enemy, remember? Both in life and in this guys-versus-girls game. Why would she look to him for help?

She drew a stick figure with a round circle at belly-height and a tiny stick figure inside it.

"Pregnant!" Stephanie shouted then looked around at the others. "No, that was not an announcement."

Madison shook her head and erased the circle but kept the smaller stick figure.

Tate was also probably drawing something — the other guys were rapid-firing responses — but Bryce's attention was caught by Madison.

"Mother!" Stephanie called out.

Madison's gaze flicked toward Bryce but didn't connect

before she turned her entire body toward Stephanie and nodded.

He laughed. He couldn't help it. 'Mother' was such an innocuous word for her to have a panic attack over.

"You guys are hopeless," Tate moaned. "My drawing is not that bad."

Bryce glanced at his brother's muddled scrawl of... something. "Yeah, it is that bad."

"Thanks, bro. I thought you were supposed to have my back."

"Only when you deserve it."

"Pretty sure that's not how families are supposed to work."

Bryce narrowed his eyes at his brother, but Tate winked. Was there a hidden message there somewhere? Right. The entirety of Sullivan Enterprises depended on family. Grandfather still ran the entire hotel empire, with Dad and Uncle Theodore managing most of the day-to-day operations from the Chicago office.

Every member of Bryce's generation was currently employed by the company, as well. Maxwell had set off to flip houses on his own for a few years, but here he was, renovating old cottages and building new ones at Sweet River. As soon as spring arrived, he'd be building tree-houses to rent out.

So, yeah, the entire clan had Bryce's back, too, even if he often felt all alone. They'd never leave him bleeding at the side of the road.

Why didn't he feel a part of things, then?

"Your turn, Bryce." Graham passed him the card box.

Yay, his favorite part. Not. He pulled a card. Whew, action and not an all-play.

Bryce picked up the marker and thought for a few seconds. How to show 'sing?' Basic head shape. Mouth in a O. Music notes... ugh, those were hard to draw. He couldn't resist adding long hair to the head while Grandfather called, "sing!"

He pointed the marker at the patriarch. "You got it."

Tate erased Bryce's drawing as Weston picked a card.

Bryce glanced at Madison, whose gaze was narrowed on him. Ah, she seemed to have noticed the long hair. Yep, he'd remembered how she used to play the guitar and sing. She had a pretty good voice, too, if he remembered correctly. He bobbed his eyebrows at her.

Her cheeks pinked as she refocused on Eryn, who shifted awkwardly with a marker in her hand.

What had Maxwell seen in that woman, anyway? Eryn was so not Bryce's type, but he had to admit she wasn't quite as nervous and strange as she'd been a few months ago. He'd poked at her as much as he could get away with just to see her squirm.

But Maxwell had stood by her every minute, easing her out of her shell until she wasn't nearly so much fun to provoke.

Yeah, yeah, those hadn't been Bryce's finest moments, but life at the ranch got so boring, especially in the offseason. The rest of the winter didn't look quite as tedious with Madison present.

His brain had looped endless versions of why she might have sought him out now, but every loop ended in the same place: no clue. Yet, she was here and didn't look to be going anywhere. Why?

He'd begun to remember the fun they'd had and the qualities that had first attracted him to her. He didn't want to remember. Didn't want to be lured back into her web.

Although there might be worse places to be.

Really? Like where?

All the ways he'd tried to push her away in the past few days hadn't had the slightest effect. And now, with several feet of snow and loss of electricity cocooning the entire staff into the lodge, pushing her away wasn't remotely possible.

Was it still snowing? Bryce needed air. He pushed off his chair and strode for the door. A phone chimed as he passed the charging station. He picked up the music-note case — Madison's? — and turned it over. Someone had texted her a bunch of photos, the visible thumbnails much too small to make out, not that it was any of his business.

He didn't mean to read the text preview. Lacey: *All of us miss you, especially Everly! Have you told...* The rest of the text was hidden.

He held up the device, still tethered to the charger. "Someone just received a bunch of photos. Good to know the cell towers are operational."

"Get out of my phone." Madison's voice was clear and commanding.

"I'm not in it." He set it back down. "I thought whoever was the recipient would want to know they had texts. Sheesh."

She marched over, eyes blazing and focused on his. "Don't touch my phone."

Bryce backed up a step and held up both hands in self-defense. "I'm not touching anything."

"Just don't." Madison unplugged the device and shoved it into her hip pocket, never breaking eye contact.

"Wow, someone is super sensitive." He studied her for a few seconds then grinned. "Maybe you want to show me those photos? Are they from your boyfriend?"

"I don't have a boyfriend."

That was good, at least. No guy would put up with his girlfriend chasing her ex. "Then you've got nothing to hide."

"None of your business."

This was getting more and more interesting. "I'm not so sure about that. You're mighty defensive about something that's none of my business." Did he dare go for it? Sure. Why not? "Who's Everly?"

If he had his guess, Madison came *this* close to punching him in the nose before pivoting and marching up the stairs. Probably going to bury that phone in her underwear drawer where he wouldn't dare dig for it.

Ha. Little did she know him.

He wouldn't, not really. But provoking the bear had been way more fun than he'd had in a long time.

She was hiding something, and he was going to figure out what it was.

CHAPTER SIX

Madison trembled in fear and anger. How dare Bryce pick up her phone and look at her texts? How dare he read the text preview? Now he knew... nothing. He still knew nothing, but with Bryce? His mental wheels were undoubtedly turning.

He might laugh and call himself the lazy, stupid member of his family, but it wasn't true. He had all the energy in the world for the things that interested him most, and an unquenchable curiosity about nearly everything. How many times had he showed her a YouTube video describing how some random thing worked?

She sank down on the edge of her bed, let the phone run its Face ID to let her in, and opened the text from her sister.

All of us miss you, especially Everly! Have you told him yet? What are you waiting for? We'll be leaving for home next week, in case you've forgotten. Dad and Nancy can stay with Everly a few extra days if needed, but she misses you, and you two need to be together.

Madison inhaled. Exhaled. She didn't want to talk to Bryce about his child. Not even a little bit. But maybe she didn't have to?

Everly was her little mini-me. She didn't look a stitch like Bryce, from her hair and eye coloring to the shape of her face. Maybe she could admit to having a child without divulging Everly's father?

Bryce would push, but he probably wouldn't suspect. Women did pregnancy math in two seconds flat, but a single guy? She doubted it. She could be vague about Everly's birthdate.

That wouldn't work for long. There were too many females around. Paisley seemed to be this big event planner and was already plotting a party for the next staff birthday.

But if Madison kept the secret close to her chest, no one would suspect. She'd lie if she had to.

Her conscience jabbed.

Okay, not a full-out lie. Just enough to divert attention. The old, 'Look! There's a spider!' trick.

She could see Jesus's sad face from here. It hadn't been that long since Madison had come to faith through her stepmom. And she already knew Dad and Nancy's opinion of whether to tell Bryce or not. And when.

It's time to tell him, sunshine.

Get out of my head, Dad.

But even her mental response to her father had weakened. It was more of a habit now.

Bryce wasn't so very terrible. She wasn't falling for him again — heaven spare her *that* fate. But he was good with his nephew, and he'd be good with Everly. If only he didn't try to cut Madison out of the picture.

Fear clamped around her heart again.

Oh, Lord, please help me to be brave. I know it's the right thing to do, but I really don't want to.

The terrible twos were yet to come, but Madison well remembered Lacey's little boy last year. Griffin had pulled off seriously impressive tantrums.

Not that different from the one raging inside Madison's head. Griffin hadn't wanted to listen to his mommy? Well, Madison didn't want to listen to Dad and Nancy. Or to God.

Tantrums never ended well.

She clutched Bunny and scrolled through the half dozen images Lacey had sent. Everly in the hotel pool with her cousins. Everly at the breakfast table, pouting. Everly blowing a kiss at the camera.

Madison could all but hear Lacey's voice. *Blow a kiss for Mama, sweetie.*

She missed her baby girl with a stab to her heart that nearly undid her. What was she doing away from her child?

A tap on her door sounded.

Madison should have locked it. She hadn't. "Who is it?"

"Me. Eryn."

Madison exhaled, long and slow. "Come in."

"Hey." Eryn entered, twisting her hands. "Is something wrong? Can I help you?"

Trust her? Or not?

Maybe it was time to open up, just a little. "Are you alone? Please close the door."

"Yes... okay." Eryn nudged the door until it latched.

"I just..." Madison couldn't do this. But wouldn't it be

easier to talk to Eryn than Bryce? A thousand times yes, but still excruciatingly difficult. "Can you keep a secret?"

"Yes, absolutely, if it helps you to have someone to talk to."

Madison wasn't sure it would. But Dad's elbow jabbed her ribs. Eryn wasn't Bryce, but this was still a step in the right direction. She opened the photo app on her phone and silently handed it to Eryn. "Scroll."

Eryn sank to the side of the bed. Her eyes widened as she swiped through a few images. "You have a daughter..." she breathed.

"I do," Madison whispered.

"What's her name?"

"Everly Louise."

"Why didn't you tell anyone? Where is she? Why isn't she here with you?"

Mr. Sullivan knew. Madison was pretty sure he'd told Tate, the resident CEO. "At the moment, she's with my sister and the rest of my family at a hotel in Jewel Lake."

"Why?" Eryn studied Madison's face. Then her eyes widened. "She's Bryce's..."

So much for thinking the partial truth wouldn't lead to the whole truth.

"Does he know? Of course, he doesn't know. That's why you're here. But you've been here five days. What are you waiting for?"

Christmas? Evidence of a new and improved Bryce? Who knew? "I'm afraid."

"Of what?"

"The Sullivans have a pile of money. What if he decides he wants sole custody? I won't be able to fight him."

"Bryce would never."

"But what if?"

"He wouldn't."

"It feels like a very big risk. You don't understand, Eryn. My daughter is my everything. I wouldn't know how to go on if he took her away from me."

Eryn set the phone down, turned sideways, and gripped both of Madison's hands. "You told me you're a Christian. Right?"

Madison gulped. "Yes."

"Let's pray about this, because I think God will give you the strength to get this in the open."

"Isn't there some other way? Maybe I should just go back to Pittsburgh and pretend this never happened."

Eryn stared at her from beneath raised eyebrows.

"I could email him from there and let him know."

"Why didn't you do that months ago?"

"I was afraid. Also, I didn't have his email address, and didn't know whom to ask to get it." Excuses.

Eryn ducked her head. "Dear Jesus, today I bring my friend Madison to You. You know her fear and understand it, but I know Your Word says that perfect love casts out fear, so please show her Your love and remove her fear. Help her to know when and how to tell Bryce he has a daughter. Help them to work things out for Everly's good and for Your good. For Madison and Bryce's good. Give Madison faith that You will work everything out, because she loves You and trusts in You. And please help me to be a good friend. In Jesus' name, amen."

Madison tried her best to swallow the lump in her

throat. "Thank you. I can't tell you how much I appreciate this."

"I'll keep praying for you, but sometimes God needs us to do the hard stuff." Eryn let out an awkward chuckle. "Ask me how I know."

"I will... some other time." Madison reached out and crushed Eryn in a hug. "Thank you. I needed a friend."

THE COLD AIR cleared some of the cobwebs from Bryce's head. He really shouldn't have snooped in Madison's phone, even though he'd meant no harm by it. Yeah, she'd overreacted, but he'd brought it on.

She was hiding something.

He had no clue what it might be, but there was something going on. She'd come West for a reason, and all he'd done was poke the bear and give her no reason to confide in him.

Maybe if he was nice to her long enough for her to spill her reasons, she'd go back where she came from. That would be a good thing, right?

But he wasn't so sure anymore. She was different than she had been, while still being the Madison he'd known and loved. Except he hadn't had a clue what love was back then. Still didn't, not really, but watching his two brothers fall in love — along with two cousins — he could see that there was a whole lot more to it than he'd figured.

These guys really cared about their wives and girlfriends in a deeper sense. Look at Maxwell, and how he'd patiently wooed Eryn until she was ready. A lesser guy —

Bryce — would have given up long before, figuring she wasn't worth it, but Maxwell was in it for Eryn's sake, not just his own.

Foreign concept, there. Bryce had taken lessons from his father, who'd put his job ahead of his wife and kids until Mom finally kicked him out when Bryce had been a young teen.

Not that Bryce wanted to work as much as Dad did. Not at all. But putting himself first before the needs of others? He was good at that part. If he didn't look out for number one, who would?

In Eryn's case, Maxwell did it. Bryce had seen the reverse, too: Eryn looking out for Maxwell and showing him there was more to life than burying himself in work.

Imagine a woman putting Bryce ahead of her own needs! Imagine Bryce caring enough about that woman — call her Madison, for simplicity's sake — to tend to her needs before his own.

Bryce didn't know how to do that. He'd been focused on himself his entire life. Third in a family of four boys, it had been hard to stand out any other way. His parents were too busy fighting to notice him. Wally had been busy being perfect. Tate was just too good-natured to think it mattered. Baby Maxwell brought up the rear, trying to please their father with his work ethic, as though it were even possible.

Bryce? He stared across the snow-covered lake beside the lodge. He'd made do with whatever scraps of attention he could find. Acting out had given him that at school and at home.

What if... what if there was more to life?

What if he could figure out how to love someone else selflessly, the way his brothers had? Even Wally and Ashley, for all their relationship had been suffering under the weight of family expectations, had been on their way to a marriage enrichment weekend when their helicopter had gone down in the Colorado mountains.

God is love.

Bryce scoffed under his breath. Too simplistic.

He heard the lodge door close then footsteps crunched toward him. Great. Someone thought he was out here sulking.

Maybe he was.

Bryce turned to see Tate. "Hey."

"You okay, bro?"

"Sure. Why wouldn't I be?"

Tate shrugged. "You've been gone a long time. I just hoped you hadn't fallen into a snowbank and couldn't get out."

"As if." Bryce snorted.

"Hey, you never know. I can't help caring about you."

"That's special."

"I agree. Having brothers is very special."

And here Bryce had said it sarcastically. Trust Tate to whoosh the wind out of his sails. "You ever miss Wally?"

"Yeah. Jamie reminds me so much of his dad sometimes. I love that kid. Don't get me wrong. But I sure wish Wally and Ashley could have stuck around to raise him themselves."

"I wasn't that close with Wally." And he would never have taken on his brother's kid and raised him as his own. He wasn't that kind of noble.

"Yeah, that five years between you two made a big difference. He was off to school when you were a baby."

"And never looked back."

Tate chuckled. "That was Wally, all right. But I didn't come out here to talk about him."

Bryce braced himself.

"I'm curious if Madison has told you why she's here yet."

He shook his head. "I have no clue. I'm not egotistical enough to think she just couldn't let go of me. I know I'm not that great a catch, like you or Max would be. I thought she might be out to punish me for some imagined wrong, but I haven't seen any signs of that. Not yet anyway."

"She doesn't seem the vindictive sort."

"Yeah, no clue. It just doesn't make any sense, you know?" Bryce turned to his brother. "You're the big shot around here. I suppose you know why she's really here."

Tate shrugged and held out both hands in a who-knows gesture. "I guess she'll tell you when she's ready."

"I wish she'd get on with it and go back to wherever she came from. Life was more peaceful before she showed up."

"She's been a big help to Eryn. I hope she stays at least until Nadine and Keith return from Hawaii."

"It's not like she can go anywhere in this mess."

"True. Oh, hey, Weston just told me that Darrell has a drone. He'll send it up in the morning and see if Highways has plowed to the Y yet. Might not need to send you to town by snowmobile if you guys only have to plow that far."

"Cool. Yeah, a drone would be epic."

"Coming back in soon?"

"It depends. Have they given up that stupid game?"

Tate laughed. "I think so. Stephanie and Paisley are making popcorn and wishing someone could play guitar and lead some singing."

"Madison plays." Drat. Bryce should have kept that inside his head.

"She does? We'll ask her when she comes downstairs."

"I don't think she brought her guitar, though." At least, he hadn't hauled it into the lodge that day.

"Stephanie has one, but she hasn't played in years. I could zip home and get it."

"I probably shouldn't have volunteered Madison."

Tate shrugged. "Let's see how it plays out. Come on back inside before you freeze your nose off."

CHAPTER SEVEN

A nd then they'd had the nerve to ask her if she played an instrument. Madison knew where *that* had come from.

Thanks a lot, Bryce.

He hadn't even been in the lodge, but Tate had gone out in the storm to find him.

She'd feigned exhaustion with a few big yawns then called it a night, ignoring Eryn's concerned gaze following her up the stairs. All she knew was she needed to not be in the great room when Bryce returned. She shouldn't have gone back downstairs in the first place, but she didn't want everyone speculating.

On second thought, let them wonder. They'd all figure it out any minute. Eryn had seen the truth in five seconds flat.

Madison paced her room like a caged animal. Felt like one, too. Trapped. Confined. Wary of whatever might come her way next, because none of the surprises so far had been pleasant.

She thumbed her phone open and scrolled through photos of her darling daughter. Wasn't having Everly in her life pleasant? Most of the time.

If only...

If only what?

If only she'd waited to have sex. If only Everly's father wasn't Bryce. If only he wasn't such a jerk.

Was he still, though? Yeah, he'd been on the rude side. After all, she'd waltzed back into his life and given him the shock of his life.

Madison snorted a mirthless laugh. Nope. The shock of his life was still to come.

Tell him, sunshine. Nothing good will come of waiting.

Get out of my head, Dad.

But... her father was right, in a way. Waiting wasn't going to improve anything. It wasn't like she and Bryce were going to fall in love for real and become a family with Everly.

Sure, that might be the ideal, in a world where the baby's father wasn't Bryce. But he was...

He wasn't so bad, really. Not that she was falling in love with him or anything, but seeing him here surrounded by his family, she could glimpse an occasional good quality. He'd been good-natured about playing games. He'd chatted with his grandfather and Eleanor for a while. He helped with the chores and seemed willing to do whatever was required to get the people and animals safely through this storm.

Okay, he wasn't all bad. But being entrusted to throw bales of hay to cows was not the same thing as being entrusted with a small child's heart and future.

He'd sat on the floor and played cars with Jamie. The kid adored him.

But Jamie adored everyone, and they him. What was not to love? He was a happy, charming child.

So was Everly.

Grr. She pivoted by the bathroom door and threw her phone back on the bed, narrowly missing Bunny. How could she tell Bryce now? There'd been little to allay her fears.

Trust Me.

This time it wasn't Dad's voice in her head but God's. She didn't want to trust. She didn't want to pry her clenched fingers off the situation, but didn't God love Everly more than her mama ever could?

That was true. Madison *knew* it was true. But, man, trusting was hard.

Trust Me.

"How can I, God?" But how could she not?

'For I know the plans I have for you,' declares the Lord, 'plans to prosper you and not to harm you, plans to give you hope and a future.'

Jeremiah 29:11. It was one of the verses her stepmother had shared with her while she and Dad had urged Madison to come clean with Bryce.

It seemed it was time to decide whether she believed God's word… or not. Oh, Lord, this was so hard.

Too hard.

Harder than being a single mother by far.

A tap sounded at her door, and she spun around to face it. Did she dare wonder who was there this time?

"It's me, Eryn. And… friends."

Madison froze, her gut the only thing capable of clenching. She certainly couldn't breathe. "Okay?"

Eryn pushed the door open. Behind her stood Paisley, Cadence, Stephanie, and Kaci. "I'm sorry, Madison. I didn't say anything, I promise. But they know something big is wrong."

"We can be very circumspect," Cadence said softly.

"We can… and we want to be your friend." Stephanie's eyes warmed. "We want to pray with you. For you."

"May we come in?" Kaci asked.

Paisley, usually the life of the party, hung back, quieter than Madison had seen her thus far.

Madison looked between them. What could it hurt to let them into her confidence? On the one hand, it could hurt a lot, but on the other hand, she hadn't had a girl-friend group since college, and most of those had drifted away when she was dating Bryce. She hadn't even told them why she left for Pittsburgh when Bryce proved he wanted nothing to do with her.

And she was going to tell Bryce, sooner or later. Would it be terrible to have a group of friends who had her back and held her in prayer?

She gulped for air. "Come on in."

They filed in, clambered onto her bed, and sat cross-legged in a circle. Paisley patted the vacant spot beside her at the foot of the bed. "Join us?"

Madison tossed a prayer heavenward before grabbing Bunny and joining the women. "I don't know where to start."

"The beginning?" Stephanie suggested.

"Madison Woodrow was born at a very early age," Paisley quipped.

That brought a few smiles but no laughter. Lightened the mood a little, though.

"Maybe not that far back," Stephanie conceded.

Here went nothing. Madison squished the stuffed rabbit to her chest. "I met Bryce around Thanksgiving a couple of years ago. We... became an item. I thought maybe we had what it took for the long haul. He didn't. He broke up with me early in January."

She could rationalize all night long. Time to cut to the chase. "To make a long story short, I figured out that I was pregnant a few weeks later."

A tiny gasp was all that broke the silence.

Who had it been? Madison didn't know. She forged on. "I tried to get in touch with Bryce, but he'd decided I was being clingy. The more I tried to find a way to tell him, the more he rejected me. Then he came here to Montana, and I cut my losses and moved to Pittsburgh, where my dad and stepmom live, along with my sister and brother-in-law. I moved into the apartment above my sister's garage, and they all helped me get through my pregnancy and Everly's birth. My sister, Lacey, has helped with childcare — she has two small kids of her own — and I figured I'd just keep being a single mom. Bryce wasn't worth tracking down *again*."

"Oh, man," Cadence breathed. "And he hasn't exactly been Prince Charming since you arrived."

"Not precisely," Madison admitted.

"So, why are you here now?" Stephanie asked.

"My dad and stepmom became Christians a few years

ago. They've been such a support to me, such an example, and they introduced me to Jesus a year or so ago. My dad has been gently nudging me to tell Bryce ever since."

"Did you ever consider email?" Kaci asked.

Madison managed a mirthless chuckle. "For five seconds, maybe, but I didn't have his address. And I need to see his face when he finds out."

"So… why haven't you told him?" Cadence asked.

Madison picked at the duvet cover. "I'm afraid he'll take Everly and cut me right out."

"He wouldn't."

"I keep telling myself that, but I haven't convinced myself."

Kaci leaned forward. "How about trying to get back together?"

"No. I can't see that working. But I sure hate to see a little kid going back and forth between her parents. I don't know. I should never have come. I shouldn't have listened to Dad."

"Was it your father's voice or your Heavenly Father's voice that finally convinced you to come?" Kaci asked.

The million-dollar question. In Bryce's case, maybe a billion-dollar question. Madison swiped tears from her eyes and shook her head. How could she know the answer?

"We need to pray together." Paisley reached for Stephanie's hand on one side and Madison's on the other. "And we need to ask God to show us how to reveal this to Bryce."

"Us?" The tiny word escaped Madison along with a little of the fear she'd held so tight.

"Us," Paisley said firmly. "We're all in this together now. Right?" She looked around the circle.

Every head nodded.

"Okay. Let's pray."

THE GLIMPSE he'd had of Madison's phone niggled at Bryce. Like, since when did she use generic photos as her lockscreen? When they'd dated, she updated her wallpaper with every couple selfie they took. She'd changed it so often he'd teased her about it.

The photo of Grant Park in Chicago on her screen now was from the city's tourism website. He knew, because a buddy of his worked in that department and had snapped it.

Was Madison purposefully hiding something behind the impersonal photo? That seemed to be a 'duh, of course' from what he knew about her.

What, exactly was she hiding?

Lacey... seemed Bryce remembered that as Madison's older sister's name. Her sister who'd married and moved to be near their dad in Pittsburgh. It wasn't weird for a sister to text her.

All of us miss you, especially Everly! Have you told...

Who was Everly? That wasn't a familiar name. A quick online search revealed it was a fairly popular female name in youngsters these days.

Bryce set his phone back on his bathroom counter and drummed his fingers as he stared at his reflection.

He shouldn't bother thinking about it. Obviously,

Madison didn't want to confide, and it likely wasn't any of his business.

But then why had she come to Sweet River Ranch?

That seemed to make it his business.

Everly.

Had he even caught a glimpse of the thumbnail photos? They'd been bright on a snowy background. Kids in snowsuits?

Bryce frowned. Why would he even think that? But one of those kids — there had been kids in the photo, right? — must be Everly.

Who was Everly?

If she was Lacey's child, she wouldn't have singled out the name in the text. That meant...

Bryce locked eyes with himself in the mirror.

It was quite a leap, but maybe it meant that Everly was Madison's child.

No. Couldn't be. If Madison had a daughter, the child would be with her, not with her sister.

Have you told...

Bryce growled in frustration. Had Madison told who what?

Him. Bryce.

But what?

That she had a child.

Had to be. But why would she think he would care if some guy had knocked her up? Was she looking for a handout? She knew the Sullivans were loaded, but did she think Bryce was a bleeding heart?

If so, she didn't know him very well. He could walk past panhandlers in the city all day long without making eye contact or feeling a ping of conscience. Just because he and Madison had slept together a whole bunch of times didn't mean he was an easy mark to get her out of trouble.

Besides, her parents had money, too. Not quite to Sullivan standards, but she wouldn't be destitute. Also, she'd had a job in Chicago. It wasn't his problem she'd left it behind.

Other than invading the ranch he called home, she hadn't made any effort to cozy up to him. Hadn't tried to rekindle a relationship. It had only been a week, though. Maybe that was phase two of her operation.

Well, he'd be ready for her. She wasn't going to suck him back into her vortex. The snowstorm had mostly blown over. Once power was restored, he'd be back in his duplex rather than this luxury accommodation. He'd stay busy helping shovel the buildings back out.

He'd keep out of her way. She'd only stay until Nadine returned — Bryce had to believe it was that temporary — and then she'd go home, realizing that he wasn't easy to sway.

Bryce had to hand it to her. She'd been so desperate to reconnect a couple of years ago in Chicago, but he'd managed to evade her. She'd disappeared to regroup before coming back at him, and she'd plotted it all out. She seemed certain she'd get him this time.

Newsflash, Madison Woodrow. I'm not that easy.

He could wait her out. This time, when she left, she'd be out of his life for good.

And he'd be alone, free to chase whichever skirt twirled in his direction. The prospect didn't excite him. Playing the field was getting old. Being alone was getting old.

He was 32. *He* was getting old, too.

Why not Madison?

Bryce shook his head at himself in the mirror. That was a big fat no. He was the one who did the pursuing, not the woman. He wasn't falling into some sort of trap.

Besides, he didn't want to hook up with a woman who had a kid. That complicated things no end. It was one thing for two people to play fast and loose, but kids made things more serious, more permanent.

Then there were those hook things Mom had talked about. Hadn't he kind of decided the next time he went for it, he'd be all in, aiming for permanent?

If he believed God cared the least bit what happened to him, now would be a fine time to pray and ask for wisdom. As it was, he had to depend on his own wits.

Too bad he wasn't 100% convinced keeping Madison at arm's length was the best way to go.

CHAPTER EIGHT

There was no point in vying for space around Weston's phone as Darrell flew the drone, but Madison couldn't stay inside, either. She wanted to know the results as much as anyone else. Possibly more than some of the others, considering Everly.

"There's the river access road." Weston shook his head. "No sign of a snowplow yet."

"What's the drone's range?" Mr. Sullivan wanted to know. "Can it go farther down?"

"Another mile or so." Darrell's thumbs manipulated the controls. "And has anyone actually phoned MDT again? Cell service is pretty solid again. I mean, it's fun to fly this thing, but a phone call would give accurate info."

"MDT?" Paisley asked.

He flashed her a glance. "Montana Department of Transportation."

No one had followed up? Madison had chatted with Lacey just last night and blown kisses to Everly. With the only charging station in a public space, she was being careful about leaving her phone downstairs for long, but she couldn't *not* charge it. It was her lifeline.

Tate and Mr. Sullivan stared at each other. Tate broke the silence with an awkward chuckle. Soon everyone laughed until tears streamed. And these men ran a billion-dollar company? They were also accustomed to all the amenities of city life.

Beside Madison, Eleanor chuckled. "That is so obvious, I can hardly believe no one thought of it."

"For the record, we did leave a message days ago. But following up is a good idea." Tate shook his head, pivoted, and headed inside.

"Where Daddy go?" Jamie tugged at Stephanie's arm.

Stephanie knelt and hugged the small boy. "To make a phone call, I think." She planted kisses on his cheeks until he struggled to get away.

The sight gutted Madison. Tears pooled in her eyes, and her arms ached with the longing to snuggle her own child. She'd never spent 24 hours apart from Everly since birth until this week. It had been way too long. As soon as the roads were cleared or at least passable, she needed a trip to Jewel Lake.

Her heart longed to gather Everly and fly back to Pittsburgh, but too many people here knew the truth now. These women wouldn't let her leave without full disclosure.

In the recesses of her mind, her father cleared his throat and gave her a pointed look.

Madison glanced at Bryce, only to catch him looking at her. He studied her as though she were a science experiment for analysis.

Her heart stuttered. Could he read her? He knew she had a secret by the way she'd reacted to him picking up her phone, but had he guessed what it was? She couldn't tell from his expression. She also couldn't look away.

He needs to know, sunshine.

Get out of my head, Dad.

Bryce circled the group, most of whom were still focused on the drone footage, and stood beside her. "So, uh, you have a kid?" He shifted from foot to foot but kept his gaze pinned on her.

Madison's heart stopped. "Why do you ask that?" *Tell him. Now.*

"Who's Everly if not your child?"

Madison gulped, and dizziness swam in her head. How could she get the words out?

Bryce shook his head and rolled his eyes. "A simple yes or no would suffice, Madison. And I'm guessing I'm right, because saying no would be easy."

"I..."

"Look, I don't know why you're here or why you're hiding her, but there's no need to sneak around. And for the record, don't bother trying to suck me into your sob story. I've never dated a single mother yet, and I'm not about to start. If you're not here to get a father for your kid, nothing else makes sense. But it's not going to work, okay? So, when the storm clears, just go home?"

He didn't know. He hadn't figured out all of it. She'd been right about guys and pregnancy math, but then he also hadn't asked the age of her daughter. Hadn't asked about the child's father or why he wasn't in the picture. Relief warred with anger that he'd think so little of her. But then, she'd been plenty eager to hop into bed with him a couple of years back.

She braced her shoulders and stared at him, trying to quench her flaming anger. "Yes, I have a daughter. Her name is Everly. You guessed my secret."

"You make no sense, Madison. Instead of trying to drag me into your problems, how about you go find the guy who knocked you up and get him involved? Or is he a pauper, and you'd rather be connected with the Sullivan money?"

Madison didn't even bother trying to hold back the venom. "Low blow, even for you, Bryce."

"What am I supposed to think?"

You could guess the rest of the truth.

A whoop went up from the people clustered around the drone's display. "The plow is on its way!" Maxwell shouted.

"Bryce? Let's get the skid steer fired up and head to meet it." Weston handed the display to Maxwell.

"Yeah. Sure." Bryce sent one more disgusted look at Madison before pivoting and following his cousin.

Madison stood immobile as the group dispersed. Their words and actions came as though through a fog. She tried to shake the murkiness from her mind, but it was impossible. How could he come so close yet leap to the wrong conclusion?

And she'd kept quiet. Again. Why? This had been her opportunity, but her tongue had been tied.

"Are you okay, honey?" Eleanor rested her hand on Madison's arm.

"I…" Madison blinked a few times. "I'm not sure."

"I know what it's like to be a single mother, you know.

Back in my day, there was a lot of stigma attached to that, but my family welcomed me home with open arms and helped me raise my daughter. Do you have support?"

Madison managed to focus on the elderly woman. "My dad and stepmom have been amazing. So have my sister, Lacey, and her husband. Lacey watches Everly when I'm working."

"Where is your little girl now?"

"At the hotel in Jewel Lake. My whole family came out here for a skiing vacation to be nearby."

The woman's eyes searched Madison's. "And you need their moral support because the child is Bryce's."

Madison closed her eyes, swaying slightly. "How did you guess? You don't even know how old she is."

"Why else would you be here?" Eleanor's arm slid around Madison's shoulders and tugged her away from the others. "Years ago, I made the choice not to tell my child's father — or anyone at all — her lineage. I felt justified because of who the man was, and I stuck to my decision for decades. Everyone but Nadine accepted my silence, but she kept pushing and pushing."

"I don't want Everly to start asking, but she will when she's bigger."

"She will, I promise you." Eleanor met Madison's gaze. "I don't think it's possible to keep that kind of secret in today's digital world. At least, that's how Nadine found her father."

"Mr. Sullivan already asked for DNA proof when I met with him last month in Chicago."

Eleanor chuckled, but not with humor. "Yes, he knows all about DNA tracking sites after Nadine. And it's too much to hope that Bryce doesn't know about them, too. Is Everly's information online?"

Madison shook her head. "I kept it private, but I shared it with Mr. Sullivan. I don't know what to do, Eleanor. You heard Bryce. He's not ready to face the truth."

"When the storm is over, why don't you bring your daughter here? Ask Stephanie if she'd be willing to watch her during your work hours. I'm sure she'd love it, and so would Jamie and Simon. That would give you a chance to see how Bryce reacted to her."

"So, you don't think I should blurt it out? Because that's what my dad thinks."

"I can't answer that for you. I only understand what you're going through, and it's hard. It's also not a secret you can keep forever, but step-by-step isn't a terrible idea."

Finally. Someone who had a clue how difficult this was.

BRYCE STARTED THE SKID STEER.

"You know what you're doing, plowing?" Weston's gloved hands twitched by his sides.

"Yeah. Don't you trust me?"

"To move gravel and haul dirt."

"We've had snow the past couple of winters."

"Not much."

Bryce's temper flared. "If you don't trust me, drive it yourself." He stood to dismount.

Weston held his hands up. "No, sorry. I'm sure you'll be fine. Really."

"Nice vote of confidence," Bryce muttered as he threw

the machine into gear. They'd both done some clearing around the ranch's parking area. Weston knew Bryce's capability. And yeah, these were deeper drifts, but the attached blower would blast the snow out of the way.

Bryce shot one more glare at his cousin as he began clearing the end of the drive. On another day, another life, he'd step back and let Weston go for it, but today? He needed something to focus on.

Madison's reaction to his confrontation irked him no end. It was stupid of her to chase him down two years after they'd broken up. It was stupid of her to hide the fact she had a child. Nothing she said or did made a lick of sense.

And he hated that he was attracted to her in the slightest. He didn't go back on breakups. Ever. She wasn't going to be the first... although she was the first to pursue him so long after the fact.

He watched the steady stream of white lofting to the side of the road, leaving a clear, albeit narrow, path behind him.

If only blasting his problems into outer space would bring similar clarity.

What was with Madison? She'd been a receptionist in a doctor's office. They had doctors in Pittsburgh, too, and it wasn't like anyone had forced her to come to Montana in the dead of winter to work in a kitchen when she could barely cook. Yet, for some reason, she'd chosen separation from her daughter to take this job.

He should have let Weston handle the skid steer. He should have tackled another area with a shovel and put his muscles into it, with less time to think.

Too late now. He was committed to a couple of hours of

road-clearing. Tonight, he'd head into Jewel Lake and... what? The old Bryce would have gone to the bar, but recently he'd decided he didn't like not being in control of himself. He'd obviously said and done things while under the influence that he couldn't recall and likely wouldn't be proud of if he could.

Nothing much besides the ski hill was open in Jewel Lake in the winter. Some of the guys went down to Creekside Fellowship on Monday evenings to a men's Bible study, but that'd be the day Bryce attended.

But of all the things he'd tried, he hadn't found satisfaction. Not really. Not deeply. His brothers and cousins seemed to think they'd found it in Jesus.

Bryce snorted, a small puff of vapor escaping into the cold, but the thought held. Was religion more than a crutch?

"It's not religion. It's a relationship," Max had said earnestly.

At the time, Bryce had snorted laughter in his brother's face. But Madison gave her faith as a reason why she'd come to forgive him. A DM would have sufficed, but maybe Jesus had urged her. If so, He was some pushy deity.

For God so loved the world that he gave his one and only Son, that whoever believes in him shall not perish but have eternal life.

No kid who'd grown up in Sunday school could miss hearing John 3:16 a few thousand times, but what was relevant about the life of a guy who'd lived millennia ago? Yeah, yeah, Bryce knew the stories of Jesus's birth, life, death, and resurrection.

Only, of course, nobody rose from the dead. Bryce's

vote would have been for his big brother, so that Wally could have raised his own kid. He would have voted for his grandmother, who'd died much too young.

Neither of them was God, though. Their resurrections wouldn't serve a higher purpose, like Jesus's. Hadn't Jesus said He'd come to offer abundant life to His followers?

Bryce's life was pathetic, not abundant. He'd once thought he had the cat by the tail, but what good had it done him? At 32, he was drifting along like a spoiled kid, working at his grandfather's beck and call with no goals of his own. He'd thought he was so smart avoiding entanglements. Peter Pan was his hero.

Yeah, he was stupid. He'd called Madison that, but it wasn't her. It was him. Maybe it was both of them.

Madison. He didn't want to be attracted to her again. He'd drawn a hard line on dating women with kids. That smelled too much of entanglement, or responsibility.

Bryce didn't do responsibility. But was there a time coming — some magic age — in which it would seem attractive?

Maybe. But that didn't mean Madison.

CHAPTER NINE

Mamamama!" Everly babbled into Madison's shoulder, her tears soaking Madison's collar.

Madison clutched her toddler close as she rocked back and forth on her knees. "Oh, baby girl. I missed you so much."

Everly sniffled, clinging tighter. "Mama."

"Not as much as she missed you, sis." Lacey sat in a nearby chair, jiggling three-year-old Griffin on her knee. "She's taken separation from you harder than I thought."

"You guys should have stayed in Pittsburgh. It's the hotel as well as separation that got to her. She's familiar with your house."

"And you know the reasons we all came. Besides, aren't you taking her to the ranch now?"

"I am." Madison couldn't begin to release Everly. "But she'll be in care there, too, with strangers. I don't know. I think we should all go home."

"Mads."

"I know, I know. But it's hard."

"I've never known someone so intent on dragging out the inevitable."

"It's not inevitable. Everly is *my* baby. What if—"

"What if Bryce loves her and is a great dad?"

Fat chance of that. But not completely impossible. Madison's conscience niggled.

"What if Bryce loves *you*?"

Madison uttered a sharp laugh. "That's easy. He doesn't. I can barely remember what I ever saw in him. Danger, maybe, and I was right."

"I'm sorry, sis, but it doesn't change the facts. You said there was absolutely zero chance she's anyone else's."

"I know." Madison closed her eyes. "Confirmed by the DNA results, in case anyone cares. Bryce's grandfather was all over the markers."

"And you said you've made friends there who guessed the truth."

Madison let out a shuddering breath. "Yes. Women are so much more perceptive than guys."

"Or maybe Bryce is being purposefully obtuse."

"Obtuse. Obtuse," Griffin repeated.

"This kid is picking up way too much," Lacey muttered.

"I have an idea…"

Lacey's eyebrows rose. "Oh, yeah?"

"Why don't you all come up to the ranch for a few days as a sort of transition for Everly? There are rooms in the lodge now that the storm is over and everyone is back in their own lodging."

"Mads, you know I love you."

Madison's heart plummeted at her sister's tone.

"But I think it's time you pulled up your big girl panties

on this one. Our flights are in two days. Yes, we could cancel our last two nights at the hotel. We could reschedule our flights, but Rob and Nancy and Dad all need to be in the office Monday. You honestly need to get this dealt with."

"You're right. I know it."

Lacey chuckled. "Can I hear that again, please?"

"Very funny." At least, it might have been if anxiety wasn't gnawing holes in Madison's stomach. "Can I bribe you?"

"Mads."

The whole family had supported her every minute. Not Mom back in Chicago, so much, but Dad and Nancy and Lacey and Rob. They'd upended their own lives to fit Everly in, not that it had been a trial as Dad constantly assured her.

But it was time, no matter if Madison resisted the inevitable by kicking and screaming. She straightened her shoulders and smoothed Everly's red-gold tangles. The little girl still had a death-grip around her neck. "Okay. I've got this."

"You're not alone, remember? God is with you every step of the way. And the rest of us will be praying for you."

"Okay."

"May I ask a question?"

"Nothing has ever stopped you yet."

Lacey laughed. "True. But I'm a little curious why you are still so conflicted about all this."

Why, indeed?

"There are only two reasons I've come up with that

make sense. One, that Bryce is a horrid guy, and you haven't said so."

"He's not," Madison whispered.

"Or, two, that you still feel something for him, and you're worried about that."

She closed her eyes, tightening her grip on her toddler. "I shouldn't."

"But you do."

"Kind of? But there are so many reasons it's a bad idea. Like he doesn't feel the same. Like he's not following Jesus."

"You told me his nephews adore him."

What was not to love about a man who got down on the floor and played cars with a three-year-old? Madison gulped for air. "Jamie is about the same age as Griff. You know how single-minded kids that age can be. Jamie is obsessed with cars, and he's a little bossy. He tells Bryce which car he may play with — always a different one — and where to drive it. And Bryce just obeys the mini dictator with a smile on his face."

"Uh huh." Lacey nodded.

"And Simon is just a few months younger than Everly. When Tate and Stephanie and the boys were staying at the lodge when the power was out, Bryce nearly always took Simon at mealtime."

"Aw, I'd have paid good money to see that."

"You can. My offer stands."

"Funny girl. Photos? I'm sure you took some."

"You know me too well." Madison settled Everly on her lap and thumbed her phone open and opened the photo app before handing it to Lacey.

Lacey whistled under her breath. "Ooooh."

"My see." Griffin yanked the phone. "Boy like me."

"Yes, that's Jamie. He's three."

Lacey looked at Madison. "He looks a lot like Everly."

"No, he doesn't."

"Uh… I hate to argue, but look at his curls and blue eyes and the shape of his chin?"

"But Everly's *my* mini-me."

"And she's also Bryce's child, and these are his nephews. Shared blood."

"They can't look alike. Everly has red hair like me, and Jamie is blond." But Madison's heart sank as she recalled some of Jamie's mannerisms.

"But they do. Everyone will see it."

"The girls already know. The guys won't notice."

"Men aren't as dumb as you think they are, Mads. And also, it's not fair to paint the whole gender with one brushstroke."

Grr. "I know."

Lacey tried to scroll, but Griffin yanked at the phone. "This kid needs bedtime, and so does Everly. Plus, Rob and Mila will be back from the pool any minute. I'm glad you're staying the night, and we'll get Everly packed up in the morning to go back with you. You'll still have a day if everything goes horribly wrong." Lacey tossed the phone back to Madison. "And you can't call it before a solid trial."

One more night of reprieve was all she was going to get.

TATE BECKONED Bryce into the storage room. "Can you help me haul this crib up to Madison's room and assemble it?"

Bryce's stomach soured. "I thought she'd left."

"No, she just went to pick up her daughter. Stephanie will watch Everly while Madison works."

"Seems like a lot of trouble. Didn't she have an entire life in Pittsburgh?"

"You could ask for her reasons."

"I sort of tried, but I'm not sure I want to know."

Tate lifted crib side rails. "That's on you, then."

Bryce grabbed the headboard and footboard. "I don't get why she's going to so much trouble, or why you all are falling in with her schemes. Don't you care that someone is trying to get her claws into your brother and siphon off some Sullivan money?"

"Dude, *ask her.*"

"I don't want to."

"You can't have it both ways."

"You know, don't you? Do me a favor."

Tate set the pieces beside the elevator. "I'm going back for the mattress."

Bryce made a face at his brother's retreating back. Tate wasn't completely wrong. If Bryce really wanted to know, if he really wanted closure, he needed to talk to Madison and make her spill her real reasons.

Hadn't he tried, though? She kept pulling back. He thought he'd guessed it and confronted her. Then she'd left in a huff.

He'd been relieved. Right? Only not exactly, because it had seemed too easy. Also, she'd been growing on him.

She'd fit right in with the other women around here, seeming to make friends with Eryn — no small feat in itself — as well as Cadence and Paisley and even Stephanie. Grandfather and Eleanor had taken to her.

Eleanor was another anomaly. The storm was over, but she was still at Sweet River, and Grandfather seemed in no hurry to return to Chicago. They took their meals in the dining hall and played endless hands of cribbage in the great room.

Tate came back down the corridor, lugging the mattress, and Bryce hit the button for the elevator. They stuffed the parts inside and rode to the second floor before hauling everything into Madison's room.

The door to her closet was ajar, revealing her clothes on the rod. The door to her bathroom also stood open, revealing toiletries on the counter. It certainly looked like she expected to return.

"Here, you hold these two pieces at right angles." Tate maneuvered the parts into place and pulled an Allen wrench out of his pocket.

Bryce held the angle. "You've done this a time or two before."

"Yep." Tate screwed in the long fasteners. "Now same over here."

It didn't take long for the unit to be assembled, then they parked it in the corner of the room.

"Are there sheets and blankets?" Bryce asked.

"Madison is bringing them."

Of course, she would. She'd obviously plotted this out in great detail.

Bryce glanced around the room and saw the stuffed

rabbit against the pillow. "Here." He tucked it into the corner of the crib.

"Nice touch." Tate grinned.

"I guess that's why she had the rabbit." Not that he'd been in her room since that first day to observe its presence.

"Probably." Tate hesitated. "I think you'll like her daughter."

Bryce rolled his eyes. "And that matters why?"

"No reason. She's a little older than Simon, and you do well with him."

"No reason, huh? This is starting to sound like a setup."

Tate looked around the room then gestured toward the corridor. "After you."

Bryce crossed his arms and leaned against the wall. "Tate. Talk to me."

"Look, bro. It's not my story to tell."

"So, you do know what's going on."

Tate backed into the corridor. "Grandfather may have let something slip."

"Slip." Bryce raised his eyebrows.

"Uh huh."

"Now it's your turn to let something slip. You know, by accident."

Tate mimed zipping his lips. "Nope."

"You're annoying."

"Your point?"

Bryce shoved off the wall and elbowed past his brother. "You're such a jerk."

Tate chuckled softly, which only caused Bryce's temper to flare. He gritted his teeth as he jogged down the staircase. No way was he responding. It was bad enough, pathetic enough, that he'd practically begged Tate for answers. He'd shown his vulnerability. His weakness.

Bryce wasn't weak. He was strong. Solitary.

Alone.

And vulnerable didn't mean wussy. Tate had always had a gentler personality, and that only seemed to help him get along with others.

Bryce was abrasive. He knew it. He'd mostly liked feeling superior to other, lesser humans. Having people cringe away from him or avoid him in the first place gave him a feeling of power.

He shoved his feet into boots, shrugged on his parka, and bolted into the crisp air. Here a guy could breathe.

Since when did he like nature? He'd hated small-town Kansas, preferring Chicago by far, even though he hadn't exactly made his father proud in the family business. It was impossible to make Dad proud. James Sullivan rode all his boys hard. Even Tate and Maxwell couldn't live up to Dad's standards. Bryce hadn't bothered trying. There were other ways to get attention.

The pristine snowbanks were only marred by the cut edges from the skid steer and shovels. Even the little lake was covered, darker spots reminding him that the layer was deceptive. Open water lay beneath the snow here and there, the ice thin.

The branches of the fir trees near the lodge were heavy with snow. Deep layers also covered the roofs of all buildings within range.

The brilliance of the sunshine glaring on the white snow made Bryce wish he had his sunglasses, but they were back in his duplex. He squinted against the brightness.

Cleanse me with hyssop, and I will be clean; wash me, and I will be whiter than snow.

Gah. Why did Bible verses from his childhood keep popping into his mind? He had no clue what hyssop was, and he cared even less. But how could anyone be washed whiter than snow?

Bryce looked around again, contemplating anything whiter or brighter than the scene around him. Impossible.

What would it feel like to be that kind of white and clean? Did he have to cling to his devil-may-care facade, or could he admit he might have been wrong once or twice?

Could he learn to care about other people instead of just himself?

People like Madison.

He shook his head. Not her. It was only those hooks Mom had spoken of that linked him to her. He'd been over her for two years. But... had he really? How many days had gone by that he hadn't thought of her once? Not many.

Why had he broken up with her? It was hard to remember. They'd had a lot of fun together. Maybe it was because she'd looked at him with forever in her eyes, and he'd panicked.

Forever didn't look so bad on Tate, though. Even Maxwell seemed to be walking with a new spring in his step the past few months as he planned a lifetime with Eryn.

Eryn couldn't hold a candle to Madison, but to Maxwell, Eryn was the sun, moon, and stars.

Bryce sighed. Maxwell would correct him on that. Jesus was all that to him. Eryn came a distant second.

Why had the nice-guy gene skipped Bryce? It might be pleasant to feel like a decent human being who liked people and was appreciated in return.

He liked Madison, even after all this. But she was bringing some other guy's child with her to Sweet River Ranch.

Why would she do that? Why would Grandfather and Tate go along with it?

Why did Bryce feel like the walls were closing in around him, even in remote, wide-open Montana?

He squinted at the dazzling blue sky.

God? You up there?

CHAPTER TEN

"Here we are, baby girl." Madison clambered out of the Jeep and opened the backdoor to release Everly from the carseat.

"Mamamama!" Everly squirmed and kicked her little legs as she reached for Madison, making it difficult to unclick the buckles.

Madison pulled the toddler into her arms, faced the lodge, and took a deep breath. Everything looked so welcoming in the bright sunshine. The wide steps had been cleared of snow and sprinkled with ice melt, ensuring they wouldn't be slippery.

God? You've promised never to leave me or forsake me. You're the only reason I'm here. Please guide me.

Well, God's promise and Dad's pushing held equal status. But last night at the hotel, after the three kids had been tucked in bed, Dad had led the adults in a prayer time asking God's mercy and guidance for Madison and Bryce.

This was the right thing to do. Maybe even today.

Madison gulped. Putting it off certainly hadn't made it

easier, but the thought of coming clean still made her wince and beg for permission to retreat.

No more, though. Today. She'd do this.

She carried Everly into the lodge then set her down to remove her boots and snowsuit. Then she hurriedly removed her own outerwear before picking Everly up again.

It was lunchtime, and voices came from the dining hall.

Eryn had assured her she'd be fine cooking a few meals on her own, now that the power had been restored and she could follow the meal plans Nadine had set out for her.

Speaking of Nadine, that woman would be back from her honeymoon in a couple of days, but Madison didn't need to talk to her before breaking the news to Bryce. She already knew it was the right thing to do, even without hearing firsthand the perspective of a child whose mother had kept the secret for over 50 years.

Here we go.

Balancing Everly on her left hip, Madison stepped into the dining hall. The space immediately quieted as everyone turned to see her.

"Madison!" Paisley called. "Let us meet your little cherub!"

Bless Paisley.

"I'm just going to dish us up some lunch and be right there."

"I'll grab a highchair." Paisley bounced out of her seat and darted toward the corner where such things were kept.

Everyone else still stared. Bryce, surrounded by some of the guys, narrowed his gaze at her.

Madison turned to the serving counter.

"She's beautiful," Eryn said softly from the other side.

"Thanks. I think so, but I'm biased."

"Can I help you? It's stew today — can she manage that okay if I put some in a small bowl?"

"I'll just spread a few pieces of mine on the tray and let her pick at it, but thanks."

"Okay." Eryn dished up a bowl. "Sourdough bread?"

"Please. Hey, that looks great. Good job."

"Thanks." Eryn flushed as she buttered a slice. "It tastes pretty good, too."

"I'm sure it does."

"Let me carry this tray. I'm sure you could manage, but I want to."

"Okay. Thanks, Eryn."

"No problem." Eryn flashed a smile as she rounded the counter and led the way to the table where Paisley and the other girls sat.

Madison tried to tuck Everly into the highchair, but the little girl sobbed and clung to her neck. They'd been separated way too long.

Fine, then. It wouldn't be the first time Madison had eaten a meal with Everly on her knee. How she was going to help in the kitchen later, she had no idea. How would Stephanie manage this toddler? No idea about that, either.

The plan had once seemed so simple. So workable. Not anymore.

"Aw, she looks so much like you, right down to the hair color." Cadence said with a smile. "What a cutie."

"Thanks." As though Madison'd had any say in her daughter's looks. She offered a spoonful of broth-laden peas and carrots to Everly, but the toddler averted her face and pushed Madison's hand away.

Great. Off to a perfect start. Everyone would get an eyeful of what a terrible mother Madison was. Hopefully no earful to go along with it. At least she'd brought a supply of squeeze-packs containing fruit and veggies. She'd offer Everly one up in their room if the toddler kept refusing.

But, for now, Everly seemed content to watch those around them while pressing hard against Madison's ribs. Conversation in the dining hall resumed, soon reaching its usual pitch. Eryn brought her own tray over and joined them, so Madison wasn't the only one just starting to eat.

These gals had her back. The back that was shielding Madison and Everly from Bryce's stabbing glares right this minute.

"Do you have a plan?" Cadence asked.

"Not really." Madison bit her lip. "I just know it has to be soon."

"We had a prayer circle for you this morning."

What had she done to deserve such solid friends? She'd only known these women for ten days! And yet, the thought of returning to a life without them — even a life that included Lacey and Rob — was terrifying. She needed them. They were sisters in Christ. A squad of women who stormed the gates of heaven for each other.

For her.

"I'll do it first opportunity. I promise."

Eryn reached over and touched her hand. "It's hard being brave. I get it. But sometimes it is seriously worth it."

She'd shared her story with Madison over the days

they'd worked together. Madison had no doubt Eryn understood, even though there was no secret of this magnitude in Eryn's past.

"Facing the past is hard anytime," Paisley agreed. "But it's often the only way forward."

"Truth," Cadence agreed. "But yes, hard."

"Does anyone know if Tate got someone to set up the crib for Everly?"

Paisley nodded. "I saw him and Bryce hauling it upstairs a couple of hours ago."

Madison nearly choked on her bite. "He made Bryce help?" What irony.

"Of course." Paisley smirked. "Tate doesn't miss a beat."

The ranch CEO was pretty solid, Madison had to give him that.

"I was kind of hoping Stephanie and the boys would be here for lunch so there would be other kids for Everly."

"I think they're planning to come for dinner." Eryn kept her voice low. "I hate to mention this, but I can't believe how much Everly reminds me of Jamie with those curls."

Madison's hand swept her daughter's head. "But Everly's a redhead like me."

"I know you think she's just like you, but the resemblance to the other side of her family is also strong."

"Genetics." Paisley offered a short laugh. "They're weird things. I don't even want to know if there are any ways I take after my sperm donor."

Madison had heard of Paisley's first meeting with her drug-addicted bio father last spring. It hadn't gone well.

Meanwhile, she wasn't going to worry about Everly's Sullivan genes. She was going to tell Bryce the truth any minute now, and then it wouldn't matter who thought they saw what.

And just like that, the small flicker of appetite she'd managed to muster fled. She might grab a protein bar later when she gave Everly the squeeze pouch. Or not.

She pushed the bowl away and gave Eryn an apologetic glance. "My stomach is churning. It's not a reflection on the food, trust me."

"Bryce is leaving the dining hall," Cadence announced quietly, looking beyond Madison.

"I'm not chasing him down."

"He's sitting down by the fireplace."

"Oh." That was different.

Was this the moment? Panic swelled in her gut. Madison looked at her friends, knowing the anxiety must show in her eyes.

"God's got this," Cadence said. "We'll be right here, praying."

"Now?" Madison felt lightheaded. "I meant today… but later."

"Now's good." Paisley met her gaze. "Cadence is right. We'll stay put."

"Imagine our hands holding you up to God," Eryn said. "We won't let you fall. Even more, *God* won't let you fall."

Madison rose, shifting Everly to her hip. She looked through into the great room. The girls were right. Bryce sat in an easy chair facing the fireplace, by himself. There would never be a better opportunity.

BRYCE STARED UNSEEING at the flickering flames. It was one thing to know Madison had a child, but it was something else entirely to observe her in mom-mode.

He flexed his fingers where they rested on his thighs. He needed to have this out with Madison, once and for all. It couldn't be good for the kid for her mother to be so agitated. To uproot her and drag her across the country, and for what?

That's what he needed to find out.

Madison's mossy green sweater and blue jeans entered his peripheral vision.

He didn't turn, but that didn't stop him from noticing her settling on the floor beside the boys' toybox and showing one of the chunky cars to her daughter.

To Everly.

The kid was a real human being who certainly didn't deserve all this trauma. Not that telling Madison so would make any difference.

"Bryce?"

Madison's soft voice registered in his brain, and he focused on her. "Yeah?"

She was pretty. She always had been. Her red hair was a couple of shades darker than her daughter's, and her face was some sort of heart-shaped with a few freckles.

The kid was cute and looked to be about Simon's size. Simon had a head of peach fuzz, but Everly had curls more like Jamie's, but redder.

"We need to talk. Is this a good time?"

Bryce snapped his gaze back to Madison's. "Oh, you're finally going to clue me in why you're *really* here?"

She bit her lip. "If you want me to."

"Please. Do enlighten me." He swept a hand.

"This is hard."

He managed not to roll his eyes. See? He was maturing.

"Bryce, Everly is your daughter."

He blinked. Stared at her. Burst out laughing.

"You don't believe me? I can prove it."

"You have *got* to be kidding me."

"I'm not. This isn't a joke, or a scam, or anything like that."

"Madison, really. How gullible do you think I am?" Although... he did know how babies were made, and he had definitely participated in that activity with Madison. "We used protection."

"And it failed."

Bryce shook his head, but he couldn't shake loose the feeling of inevitableness as things clicked into place. She'd talked to Grandfather in Chicago. He'd known when he hired her. Tate must have known. Probably everyone knew but him.

It still had to be an elaborate trick. Didn't it?

"DNA?" That was how Aunt Nadine had convinced Grandfather.

"Her DNA matches yours, Bryce. Your grandfather verified it. The timeline matches, to say nothing of the fact that I hadn't been with anyone but you. She was born September 22nd. It takes nine months—"

He surged to his feet. "Do you think I don't know that? I'm not stupid, Madison."

"I didn't say you were."

Bryce could feel her gaze on his back as he stared out the wide window at the snow-covered lake. He had a child?

It couldn't be. But Grandfather was no easy mark. He'd kept control of a billion-dollar empire into his 80s. The old man was as sharp as a tack, and nothing got past him. If Grandfather had verified the DNA results, then... Bryce was a father.

He pivoted.

Madison sat on the floor, the little girl pressed back against her. Both had identical green eyes, both focused on him with visible apprehension.

"You're serious."

She bit her lip but nodded.

"Why didn't you tell me?" The accusation came out even harsher than Bryce intended. He winced.

She did not. "You may recall that I tried."

All those times he'd called her clingy. Unwilling to let go, as though he were some sort of stellar catch, and she was a leech. What a pompous fool he'd been.

"There's email." Not that he'd have opened one from her.

"There is." But her agreement did not sound like concession.

"You could have had Grandfather let me in on it." Even as he said it, he knew that would have been a terrible idea. He already felt like a recalcitrant schoolboy in the old man's presence. How much worse if that's how he'd received the news. But Grandfather had known for at least a month. Kudos on his ability to keep a secret.

Madison didn't answer. She just looked at him, soothing the child in her lap. Probably didn't even realize she was doing it.

"What do you want from me?"

"I only felt it was right for you to know."

"There's a catch. There has to be. You're after money."

"Do you really think so little of me?"

Bryce raised his eyebrows. "Sullivans have plenty."

"I know. But I make a decent income. We'll be okay. It's not about money."

Wasn't it always? Power came from wealth. He shook his head. "Okay, fine. If it's not about money, then what? Just your conscience getting the best of you?" Because he could have lived without that.

But this child was his flesh and blood. He did need to know. What should he do with that information? No clue. The knowledge didn't make him into some sort of Super Daddy.

Tate had become a father by taking on their dead brother's son. What a great guy he was. Bryce still felt the bitterness at everyone comparing him to his good-boy brother. But if Tate could love Jamie as his own, couldn't Bryce learn to feel something for a child he'd helped create?

"I was afraid you'd hire a lawyer, take custody, and cut me right out."

He snorted. As if. What would he do with a child? He knew a lawyer all right, though Aunt Bridget was a corporate attorney, not family law. But no. "I'd never do that."

"Good." Relief slid across Madison's face. "I'll hold you to that."

She'd truly been worried? "Look... I don't know what to say. I need some time to think." He turned back to the window.

"Bryce?"

"Yeah?"

"Sit down here. Please look at her. She's yours as much as mine, as much as it pains me to admit it. Don't reject her."

"She's just little. She doesn't know stuff like that."

"Kids are more sensitive than you think. Please, Bryce."

Bryce had been 14 when his dad had quit pretending to be a family man, left their Kansas home, and moved to Chicago full-time. But the rejection had been present Bryce's entire life. He'd never been good enough to draw his father's attention. Even rebelling hadn't done the trick.

Not having a dad who cared about him had left a gaping wound in his life that remained.

Aunt Nadine had spent her entire life wondering who her father was. From what she'd said, the thought had consumed her every day.

Bryce looked at the little girl sitting in her mother's lap.

Could he do that to his own child?

He wasn't daddy material!

But genetics didn't care.

CHAPTER ELEVEN

Madison bit her lip as she watched Bryce shift from foot to foot. What was he going to do? There was that deer-in-the-headlights look.

She could hardly blame him, honestly.

Everly reached for the car in Madison's other hand. "Voom." She'd probably learned that from Griffin.

"Yes, sweetie, that's the sound a car makes. Want to drive it?" Madison tried to set Everly on the floor beside her, but that was a no-go.

Movement in the dining hall beyond Bryce caught her attention. Cadence made a praying-hands sign, and the others nodded.

God had this. He did.

Madison took a few deep breaths with her eyes closed. When she opened them, Bryce was looking at her. "Please sit down, Bryce."

There was an entire battle going on in his tortured gaze, and her heart went out to him. He truly had not suspected a thing, and she'd dropped a bombshell that would change the trajectory of his life, unless he walked away without a backward glance. Even then, it couldn't help making an impact.

He knew now.

Bryce scrubbed a hand through his hair. "Madison, I don't know what to say."

"Start by sitting down so I don't get a crick in my neck."

He took a couple of steps closer before dropping to the stone hearth. "I'm sitting."

"Now talk to me."

He shook his head. "I don't know what to say. I want to scream. I want to deny. I want a stiff drink. I want... everything and nothing. I want this to be a bad dream."

Madison winced. Well, she'd asked him to talk. "I think that jumble of thoughts is probably pretty normal in such a situation."

He scoffed. "You think?"

She had no reply.

"I quit drinking, by the way."

"Good choice." They'd both drank to excess in the old days. "Why?"

Bryce shrugged. "I decided I didn't like not remembering what happened."

"Right." She'd quit the minute she suspected pregnancy.

He leaned forward, elbows on his knees, his hands clutching the back of his bowed neck. After a long moment, he glanced over at her. "Where do we go from here?"

"That's up to you."

"I'm not marrying you."

"I'm not asking you to. Shotgun marriages are such an outmoded idea. Marriage needs to be based on something much more solid."

His eyebrows flicked up. "Like?"

"Common faith and goals. Love. Commitment not made under duress."

"Like Tate and Stephanie."

"They seem a good example, but I don't know them that well."

"It was fast for them. They barely knew each other. We all thought it was a joke at first."

"They seem to be making it work."

"Yeah." Bryce shook his head again, looking down. "Your kid…"

"*Our* daughter's name is Everly Louise Woodrow, but your name is on her birth certificate."

His head jerked up. "It is?"

"I knew, Bryce. There was never any doubt. You were the only man I ever slept with."

"I should never have been left in the dark."

"I did try to tell you. You know that."

His sigh came from deep within. "You did. I'm not sure what to say now. I'm sorry? But I'm not sure what I would have done with the information two years ago."

"I felt my conscience was clear. I'd tried several times to talk to you and got the brush-off. So, I figured I'd just raise her myself. Plenty of single moms have no support from their child's father."

"And that changed because…"

"Because I became a Christian. We talked about that the day I came."

Bryce's nod looked grim. "When you told me I wasn't one."

Maybe she'd been too hard on him. But had she? "Yes, that day. My dad and stepmom started encouraging me to talk to you when I gave my heart to Jesus. They've been in Jewel Lake along with Lacey and Rob and their two kids since I came here, keeping Everly with them at the hotel. And praying for me. For you."

His eyebrows rose. "They're praying for me?"

"They care about you. You're the father of a child they love and are related to."

"This is wild."

"I know." A few ranch residents filed by, glancing toward the fireplace, but not interfering. Paisley offered a thumbs-up on her way past.

"I need time to think."

Madison nodded. "That's reasonable. Thanks for not walking out on this discussion."

Bryce laughed, but not like he found it funny. He rose and stuffed his hands in his jeans pockets.

He'd never worn jeans in Chicago, but they looked good on him. Not that she should notice.

"You know..." He braced his shoulders. "Maybe we should try."

"Try what?"

"Marriage." He poked his chin toward Everly. "It's not fair to her this way."

Madison narrowed her gaze. "Are you seriously proposing to me like that? Not a chance, buster."

"You can't deny it would be better for her."

He had yet to say their daughter's name and still presumed to know what was best?

Madison shifted Everly and surged to her feet, holding the toddler. "I can absolutely deny that it would be best for her. That is not what marriage should be based on."

"Are you turning me down?"

"You're mocking me." She spat the words at him.

"I'm not. I'm just trying to figure out the path."

"Keep trying. That's not it. Not like that."

Bryce rolled his eyes. "Women. I can't figure you out."

"We are not going to make any hasty decisions. I know you haven't been a praying man—"

"Who said?"

"You basically did when you equated sitting in a pew for an hour a week with being a Christian. *As I was saying*, it's time for you to pray. God is the only one who can give us the direction we need."

"If I thought He cared, I'd pray."

She stared at him.

He stared back.

Were they getting somewhere? "Why don't you think He cares?"

Bryce waved a hand. "Look at the mess the world is in. Wars. Natural disasters. Pandemics. If God ever cared, it's obvious He washed His hands of this planet a long time ago."

"Our messy world is why Jesus came," she said softly. "We still make our choices, but now there is hope."

"I wish I could buy it. I really do."

"That's why I'm praying for you."

He shook his head slightly. "Religion doesn't have to come between us."

"I'm sorry. I'm not starting out on that foot. Both of us come from divorced families. I'm not going into an unstable relationship knowing it's doomed from the start."

Bryce glowered at her.

Madison let out a long breath. "My parents split when I was ten. It was awful... although better than hearing them fight all the time, I guess."

"My parents only fought when my dad was home, which was almost never. Work consumed him."

"And then he left completely," she said softly. "You felt like he abandoned you kids along with your mom in one fell swoop."

"Because he did."

"So, let's not do that to Everly."

"CAN I TAKE KENNEDY OUT?" Bryce asked Weston.

"No. The snow's too deep."

"He probably needs exercise." Bryce certainly needed something to clear his head, and a gallop on his favorite gelding sounded perfect.

Weston shrugged. "It's not safe."

"I'll go down the road."

"It's icy."

Bryce growled in frustration. "So, you're just going to leave the horses locked up in the stable until spring?"

Weston stuck his thumbs through his belt loops. "If needed, sure, but the snow is likely to melt down to manageable proportions in the next couple of days. I'm not risking one of the horse's necks so you can have some pleasure."

"It's not for pleasure."

Weston's eyebrows peaked under his cowboy hat. "Even worse."

"Look—"

"No, *you* look. If you need some fresh air, take out some of the snowshoes or cross-country skis."

"Too slow. Maybe a snowmobile?"

Weston shook his head. "I can't stop you, but know this. You can't ride fast enough to get away from whatever's bugging you."

"What do you know about that?"

"Saw you and Madison having a heart-to-heart by the fireplace a bit ago. Doesn't take a genius to figure out what's going on."

"And that is…?"

"You're the father of her kid."

Had everyone but him seen the light? He gritted his teeth.

"You wanna talk?"

To the surly cousin he'd only known for two years? Not a chance, though Weston hadn't been so bad once Bryce had gotten to know him. At least, after Paisley got through to him.

"Makin' a guess here, but it's probably God you're fighting against, not Madison so much."

"Great. Someone else who knows me better than I know myself." Bryce didn't even try to keep the sarcasm out of his voice.

"Am I wrong?" Weston asked mildly.

Totally wrong. But the words refused to come out of Bryce's mouth. He might be confused about a lot of things. He might be a lazy butt riding on the family fortunes, but he wasn't generally a liar.

"Looks like a cute kid."

"Sh-she looks a lot like Madison." Which, by definition, made her cute.

"What's her name?"

"Everly." This was the first time Bryce's mouth had uttered his daughter's name. He had a daughter.

Weston nodded. "Nice name."

"I guess." Not like Bryce had had any input. "Her birthday is September 22." Why had he added that? No clue.

"Are they still going to be here on her birthday?"

That was eight months away. Anything could happen. What did a little kid's party look like, anyway? Stephanie generally invited the entire Sullivan clan, her parents, and half the staff to celebrate the boys.

Everly's first birthday would have been in Pittsburgh a few days after Graham and Cadence's wedding here. Only Madison's family and friends would have been present. The other half of Everly's family hadn't known she existed.

Part of Bryce wished he still didn't know. Hadn't life been simpler before this information had sluiced over him with no warning like a bucket of ice water?

The other half of him was sort of in awe. Maybe this was a good excuse for embracing adulthood, but he didn't even know how. He'd been drifting his entire life.

"...or you could fly out for her birthday, I guess."

With a start, Bryce realized Weston was still talking. "Fly out?"

"Well, Madison is from back East, right?"

Would Madison consider leaving Montana and taking Everly with her? Why not? Bryce hadn't given her any reason to stay, other than blurting out they should get married. He cringed. Not his finest moment, but still, wasn't it one of the options?

How many options are there?

"She stays here, you move there, you pass Everly between you, or you default."

Bryce shook his head. He must've asked that out loud. And Weston was correct. The options were simple. "I can't move to Pittsburgh. She'd be crazy to ask that of me."

"Has she? Asked, I mean?"

"No. We... didn't get as far as logistics. I'm still trying to grasp the fact that I have a daughter."

"That's a good thing."

"What?" Bryce scowled at his cousin.

Weston cracked a grin. "Until now, I thought Sullivans could only father boys. Paisley wants half a dozen kids, and I'm not sure I'm up for raising six sons."

Bryce snorted a laugh. "That's a lot, all right."

"It is. I might be able to talk her back by one or two, but right now, she's pretty adamant." Weston grinned. "I think she'll be a great mom."

Suddenly Bryce could see Weston setting a little kid — a curly-headed girl like Everly, maybe — on a horse's back. "I think you'll be a good dad, too." No matter that their wedding was still months out.

"You think?" Weston scratched his head then replaced

his hat. "I wouldn't have thought so a couple of years ago. I guess if there's hope for me, there's hope for you."

Bryce studied Weston's face. "I don't know how. My dad was never home. He never took me to Little League... or anywhere, really."

"Me and my dad butted heads all the time. Can't say I learned the best way to take care of kids from him, either."

"But you're not afraid of it?"

Weston shook his head slowly. "Not anymore. Paisley makes the difference. And God."

Of course, God. "How so?"

"Because He's basically the ultimate Father. I've been going to a study on the kind of Father He is down at Creekside Fellowship Mondays. You should come."

"Nah. No one wants me."

"I do. And yeah, it already started, but we all missed last week on account of the storm. Most important, don't you think you owe it to Madison and Everly to figure this parenting thing out?"

If Bryce were going to be the kind of father his dad was, then Madison might as well return to Pittsburgh. Bryce would send money and birthday and Christmas gifts if he remembered. He could try for a relationship when Everly was older, because face it. There wasn't much to do with a kid the age she was now.

But that wasn't how being a father worked. Dads — good dads, not ones like James Sullivan — were there day in and day out. They took the night shift if the baby was sick. They heated bottles and changed diapers and knew how to buckle carseats.

Could Bryce let Madison take Everly back to Pennsylvania?

No. Not without him. Not without giving him a chance… even though she'd shot down his proposal.

Bryce winced.

That had been an epically stupid move. What had he been thinking?

CHAPTER TWELVE

I'm sorry." Madison clutched her sobbing child to her chest. "I don't know what to do with her. She's not letting go."

"I can manage dinner." Eryn looked between Madison and Everly. "Have you invited your family for tomorrow yet?"

"I did. They'd love to come, if you're sure Mr. Sullivan won't mind. Please tell me what we owe for four adults and two kids for a meal."

Eryn waved a hand as she shook her head. "Nothing. And, yes, that's what Mr. Sullivan would say, too. They're your guests."

"If you're sure. They're flying back Sunday." Without Madison. Without Everly.

Panic threatened to overwhelm her, or maybe it was the stranglehold of Everly's arms and legs from around her body. Her daughter was absolutely not letting her out of her sight... or grasp.

"Nadine will be home tomorrow night and back in the

kitchen Monday. I can get Paisley or Cadence to help while Everly settles in."

"But I have to earn my keep!"

Eryn cracked a grin. "Rumor has it that Stephanie lived at Sweet River for several months simply as Jamie's nanny. She didn't have another job."

"But…" How did that relate?

"Jamie is a Sullivan grandchild, and he needed a caregiver while Tate worked."

"Uh huh?"

"Everly is a Sullivan grandchild, too. She needs a caregiver." Eryn tapped Madison's shoulder. "She needs you."

Madison shook her head. "But that's not how it works."

"It could work that way. I could talk to Mr. Sullivan about it."

"You can't do that."

"Sure can. He's really nice, you know. He cares about everyone here, not just the immediate family." Eryn gave her a pointed look. "And you're immediate family."

"But I'm not married to Bryce."

"Would you if he asked?"

Madison snorted a laugh. "He already did, and I said no. It came right on the heels of him saying he *wasn't* marrying me because of Everly."

"That's confusing."

"Tell me. I think the news scrambled his brain and he didn't know which direction was up."

"I guess that's understandable, all things considered."

Madison rubbed Everly's back as the toddler's sobs settled to occasional hiccups. "Yeah, it is. I don't see marriage as much of an option, honestly. A lot of things would have to change."

"God's in the miracle business, you know," Eryn said softly. "I sure never expected to move to Montana, start a new life, and be loved by an amazing man like Maxwell."

"You guys are adorable together."

"Thanks. But the fact that it's all a miracle still stands. I've told you my story."

Madison nodded. "My family and I have been praying for Bryce for the past year, and I guess our job isn't over yet. His spiritual walk is far more important than whether he and I get back together. At this point, it's not even what I want."

Which was a bit of a lie, if she let herself dwell on it. A happy home where both parents loved God and loved each other would definitely be in Everly's best interest, but it seemed too big a stretch to see the other parent as Bryce.

Maybe now that the secret was in the open, Madison could meet some great guy who'd love her and her daughter, and Bryce could be sidelined as a distant parent.

If that happened, she wouldn't stay in Montana, but she felt she needed to now while Bryce was in limbo. And honestly? That whole Norman Rockwell scenario didn't seem attractive unless she pictured Bryce as her partner. But could he step up and become the man she needed him to be? The man of faith God desired him to be?

"She's falling asleep on your shoulder," Eryn whispered. "What a sweetheart."

"She'll wake up the second I try to lay her down."

"Then don't. Go sit in one of those chairs in the great

room with her, and I'll bring you a cup of tea and a couple of cookies. I can manage dinner tonight."

Sounded so tempting. "If you're sure."

"Absolutely."

Madison's phone pinged as she turned into the other room. She settled into a deep chair and arranged Everly against her before checking the message from Lacey.

How did it go?

That was a loaded question. How to reply? Hmm. *He knows now. He took it about as well as expected.*

Does he believe you?

Yes, but he's not happy about it.

Can't wait to meet him. I'll set him straight. [glaring emoji]

Madison huffed a laugh. Poor Bryce didn't even know yet that he'd be subject to her family tomorrow. He'd met her mom a couple of times in Chicago, but never the Pittsburgh crew. Mom had been horrified at Madison's pregnancy and probably hadn't told a single one of her friends. She wasn't that involved with Lacey's kids, either, and Lacey had been married to Rob before getting pregnant. Mom wasn't grandmother material.

Don't be too hard on him.

Who? Me? [laughing emoji] He deserves the third degree.

He needs prayer, not judgment.

Look at her, being all spiritual. But it was still true. He was outside somewhere right now, no doubt kicking himself in the pants all around the ranch.

Madison knew how that felt. She'd scolded herself over and over in the early days of her pregnancy. It had taken her months to believe anything good could come from the condition she'd found herself in.

But then God had slipped past her defenses and shown her His great love and forgiveness.

I know you're right, but it's gonna be hard.

I get it.

Mila and Griffin are begging for the pool. TTYL.

Give them hugs from Ev and me.

Will do.

Madison turned her phone over and closed her eyes.

"Here's your tea — decaf chai with cream, just how you like it. And two of those pumpkin chocolate chip cookies you made a couple of days ago. They're scrumptious."

She looked up to see Eryn setting a cup and saucer within reach. "Thank you. I don't deserve a friend like you."

Eryn grinned. "Friendship is a great blessing."

So true. Madison deserved no good thing. No one did. But God gave beautiful gifts, anyway.

She could only pray Bryce would come to see Everly as a gift.

BRYCE HAD THROWN his entire being into hauling hay for the horses and cows through the storm. Even now, the snow made getting around the ranch harder than before. They'd plowed and blown it aside, but there was still so much clogging the area that today he used a shovel for the sheer exertion of it.

He didn't know what to do besides heavy labor. It kept him too busy to sit around watching his daughter and her mother and too tired to think about his next steps. At least, he'd hoped to be too tired to think, but the visions of

Madison sitting on the floor cradling Everly in her lap, both of them watching him with identical apprehensive expressions slipped to the forefront at every opportunity.

Maxwell had given him a heads-up that Madison's family was coming for the afternoon and staying for dinner.

She should have told him herself.

Not that he'd allowed himself to be found by her since he'd walked out of the lodge yesterday afternoon. He'd blocked her number two years ago and hadn't bothered to unblock it.

He had no one to blame but himself for being the last to find out. He had no one to blame but himself for a lot of things, the list too long to even get started on.

Half of him wanted to drive to Jewel Lake and get takeout from the Golden Grill, neatly avoiding the Woodrow clan. Half of him wanted to hide in his duplex and eat peanut butter on stale crackers.

Zero of him wanted to enter the dining hall at 5:30 and meet her family in front of his, never mind everyone who knew him.

Man up, Bryce. It's time.

Even Peter Pan eventually had to face what his immaturity had done to Neverland.

So... Bryce didn't need to wait until dinnertime. He could shower and show up at the lodge ahead of time. He could seek Madison and her family out.

Now, there was a concept.

If he were praying these days, he'd ask God for wisdom. For strength. But he'd never been on particularly close terms with the Almighty. Somehow, he'd become God's shirt-tail relative. His grandfather, his mom, his brothers, his cousins… everyone seemed to be best buds with God. Not Dad, so much, but Bryce didn't have to see much of his paternal unit these days. A big plus to living in Montana. Some would call it a blessing.

He shoved the tip of the shovel into a snowbank near his door and looked up at the blue, blue sky. "You there, God?"

No one answered.

Of course, no one answered. What had Bryce expected? A booming voice from the sky asking what He could do for Bryce today? Sort of like Estelle at the Golden Grill, taking an order then bringing it out, hot off the grill, ten minutes later?

Bryce shook his head and went inside, where he shed his outerwear and got himself cleaned up. A bit later, wearing a crisp, clean pair of jeans and a forest green Henley, he looked himself in the mirror. Time to shave off the scruff he'd ignored over the storm, though Madison hadn't said anything about it.

He paused, hand on his razor. Now he was deciding whether to shave or not based on Madison's reactions? He had it bad.

He could deny it all he liked, but he wasn't over her. He hadn't been over her in the entire two years since he'd broken up with her. Why, again, had he done that?

Oh, yeah, he'd been afraid of commitment. He'd seen wedding bells in her eyes, so it had been time to shut that right down.

Too late.

Ironic, huh?

Fact remained, he did care what she thought, and he wasn't sure what to do about it. He'd messed up yesterday. Reacted like an idiot. Laughed at her, rejected her, then made a half-hearted effort to redeem himself by offering to marry her.

Yeah, he might not be the brightest crayon in the box, but even he knew that had been pathetic to the point of insulting. No wonder she'd shoved a fierce, quick 'no' into his face.

Did he really want her back? Did he want to be a father to his child?

The thought still made his brain slide sideways. He, Bryce Daniel Sullivan, was a father. He had a little girl, a daughter who needed a daddy.

He took a deep breath, squared his shoulders, and looked himself in the eye. It couldn't possibly be that difficult to be a better dad than his own had been. Being a husband? That sounded complicated, but he didn't have to marry Madison to be a father to Everly. He could do his best to steer clear of any entanglement with his child's mother.

After all, Dad had failed as a husband first. His sons had been collateral damage to a failed marriage. So... if Bryce didn't marry Madison, then he could focus on the most important part of this equation.

Everly Louise Woodrow.

He was listed on her birth certificate, even though she didn't carry his surname. Today wasn't the day to ask about changing that. Maybe he needed to earn the right.

Ya think, Sullivan?

Right. He had a family to meet. A family who had been

with Everly ever since her birth. A family he needed to win over as best he could.

He had one goal for the next eighteen years, and that was to be the best father this kid could ever want or need.

His gut quaked. He had zero idea how to accomplish that. Hadn't Weston said something about a men's group at the church? Could Bryce really let a bunch of religious yahoos into his life?

Maybe they weren't yahoos.

Maybe they were ordinary men like his brothers and cousins who simply wanted to be better leaders. Better men.

If one thing had become perfectly clear over the past 24 hours, it was that Bryce somehow needed to become a better man.

The old Bryce needed to be given the boot to make room for Bryce 2.0.

Could he reinvent himself without God? Did he want to try?

CHAPTER THIRTEEN

Bryce straightened the neck of his Henley, though it probably didn't need it. He resisted the urge to pat his gelled hair.

Right now, if he were the praying sort, he'd be asking God for... what, exactly? Guidance. Favor. Forgiveness, maybe? Maybe God guided other people. Maxwell was certain God did. Bryce wasn't so sure. The world seemed rife with random coincidences.

Thinking about God wasn't addressing the issue at hand. He raised his hand and rapped on the door of the activities room. It was a public space — he could walk right in — but it was where Eryn said Madison and her family were meeting.

The door swung open, and Madison's surprised gaze met his. "Bryce?" Her voice quaked.

The suave, cocky Bryce had fled. Probably just as well. He did manage a smile, though it likely looked pained. "One and the same."

"Oh." She bit her lip and glanced over her shoulder. "Come on in."

"If you want me to leave, just say so."

"No. This is probably for the best." She pulled the door wide and beckoned him as she turned to face the room's occupants. "Bryce, this is my dad, Allen Woodrow, and my stepmom, Nancy. My sister Lacey, her husband Rob, and their kids, Mila and Griffin. Everyone, this is Bryce Sullivan." She paused for a nanosecond. "Everly's father."

Bryce tried to meet the gazes of everyone as Madison introduced them. He nodded and smiled, but all he wanted to do was flee. Where was the devil-may-care Bryce of years gone by? Maybe it was a good thing that guy wasn't in the room.

He rocked on his heels and stuffed his hands in his jeans pockets. "Hi."

Allen was the first to recover. He strode across the room and offered his hand to Bryce. "I'm pleased to meet you. I'm glad you came by."

Nice somebody was. A swift glance at Madison proved she didn't agree.

"Nice to meet you, sir. And, uh, thank you for taking care of Madison and Everly." Bryce shook the man's hand firmly.

"It was our pleasure, but I'm glad you're in the picture now."

"Dad…" Madison growled in a threatening whisper.

"It's true, sunshine." Allen grinned at Bryce. "I've been after her for a while to track you down. A man deserves to know he has a child."

"I agree."

Bryce could see where Madison had inherited her red hair, though Allen's was shot through with gray. That was about where the similarities ended.

A woman who looked more like Madison approached. "Lacey Davidson. I'm with Dad. It's about time. Come on in and have a seat."

Madison glowered at her sister.

That chair was going to be the hot seat, but a guy in Bryce's boots had to get through this before life got simpler again. Would it ever? His gaze swept to a corner of the room where a girl of about five and a boy Jamie's size played with a toy kitchen, while Everly pretended to drink from a plastic cup in between giggles. She was a far cry from the sobbing mess Bryce had encountered just yesterday.

She knew these people. Felt safe with them.

She didn't know her own father. That was Madison's fault.

He sighed. No, it was his fault. Man, he hated taking responsibility for stuff, but here he was, and that little kid needed a dad. She needed *her* dad. The situation wouldn't go away if he had a stiff drink. It wouldn't go away if he went to Mexico for a week or a month.

It wouldn't go away.

He was a father, and this was his child.

How had Dad managed to walk away from four sons with barely a glance over his shoulder? Maybe that wasn't fair. The boys were always welcome to visit Chicago and sit in the corner while Dad solved hotel crises on the phone. He had taken them on a few 'vacations' with a nanny, mostly to Sullivan hotels in other countries, where

Dad worked while the boys played in the pool. And still, all four them had followed him to Chicago after high school, leaving their mother behind in Kansas.

He needed to make that up to Mom somehow.

Bryce blinked the room back into focus. Letting his mind wander was not going to help.

"So, tell me about yourself, Bryce. Your grandfather owns Sweet River Ranch, is that correct? What's your position here?" Allen leaned forward on his elbows.

"Yes, this is my grandfather's ranch. I... I'm head of landscaping." Not as prestigious as Tate's CEO position or Maxwell's head of building and renovation projects, but it was what it was.

"I'm sure the grounds are very beautiful in the summer."

"Yes, sir, they are. The mountains, the lake, and the trees make a stunning backdrop."

"Small lake compared to what you're used to in Chicago," Rob put in with a grin.

"Very small, yes. Our guests love to swim and paddle kayaks. That sort of thing."

"A ranch. Do you ride horseback a lot?" This from Lacey.

"A couple of times a week through the season, when I have time. More in the offseason, but not when the snow's this deep."

"I'd love to see the stables this afternoon, if we have time. Madison and I enjoyed riding when we were kids."

Madison shot her sister an indecipherable look.

Bryce nodded. "I'm sure that could be arranged. The corrals have been shoveled out. We could probably get the kids up on one of the ponies for a few minutes, if

Weston has time. That's my cousin who's the chief wrangler here."

Lacey's face lit up. "Mila would love that! She's so into her My Little Ponies."

Whatever that was. Sounded like a toy, maybe? Bryce was going to get a crash course in what was popular with kids these days. Man, all this was so daunting.

Your running days are over, Bryce Daniel Sullivan.

It took a force of will to keep that in the forefront.

WHY HAD Bryce crashed these last hours together before her family flew back to Pennsylvania? Madison had meant to point him out at dinner, not invite him in for a meet-and-greet.

It could only mean one thing, that he was serious about stepping into Everly's life. Which, by default, meant Madison's life. In the past couple of weeks, she'd seen glimpses of the Bryce she'd fallen for two years ago. He'd changed some, and she'd changed a lot. She hadn't expected there to be any glimmers of attraction given the way he'd ditched her and blocked her. She'd thought she was over him.

She'd been wrong. Apparently old neurological pathways were still intact, but that didn't account for the emotions she felt right now, watching and listening to him chat with Dad and Lacey. There was no precedent for this. He'd hadn't been chatty with Mom the few times they'd met back in Chicago. Now, he was all relaxed and pleasant. It was hard to remember why she should keep him at arm's length.

He wasn't a believer. That was the big one.

Also, he couldn't be trusted. Not after how he'd tired of her before... but God could fix that.

Dad and Nancy had been praying for Bryce's salvation for two years. Madison hadn't been, to her shame, even after she became a Christian herself. Why? Was it that she didn't think God could get through to him, or that she didn't want to have to figure out how to feel about a new and improved Bryce?

Forgive me, Lord.

With him embracing his position with Everly — at every lull, his gaze drifted to watch their daughter — their lives would be entangled for decades to come. All their lives, really. They'd both attend her graduations, her wedding. They'd both be grandparents to Everly's future children. Wouldn't all of that be a whole lot easier if they were friends?

Not lovers. Not a married couple.

Only friends.

But could she do just friends with Bryce when she still felt this attraction to him? Paisley spoke of his landscaping abilities with praise. Maxwell seemed to enjoy visiting with him at the dinner table. He was respected here, it seemed, but the kicker had come when she'd seen him on the floor playing cars with Jamie and helping Tate with Simon during those evenings of the storm.

Her gaze had been drawn to his during games nights... and his had been drawn to her, it seemed.

Did he have regrets? How would she respond if he offered a heartfelt apology? He kind of already had, but she'd brushed it aside along with that pathetic proposal.

He'd been in shock. She got that. She'd never take advantage of anything he said in a moment like that.

But maybe… maybe some of it was real.

Ever the needy one, Griffin brought a red toy car to his dad. Rob gestured toward Bryce. "Show him."

Bryce turned to the little boy with a grin. He leaned closer and listened to Griffin's excitement.

Madison couldn't hear the words. Griffin usually spoke quickly and not that clearly while jiggling in place. But Bryce seemed to say all the right things and remained focused on Griffin for much longer than she expected.

Bryce could become Griffin's uncle. He could become part of this family group, not merely a visitor she hadn't invited and hadn't wanted present.

But what if she opened herself to that possibility and Bryce rejected her again? How could she trust him not to break her heart twice?

Fool me once, shame on you. Fool me twice, shame on me.

But… God.

Not that Bryce was in tune with God, but she was trying to be.

Forgive him from your heart.

That's a tall ask, Lord.

Forgive him, and let Me handle the rest.

Madison surged to her feet and strode to the window, tears tingling in her eyes. Was God making this a matter of trust? Was this a pivotal moment in her new spiritual life? Was she required to extend true forgiveness?

Yeah, she'd told Bryce that's why she'd come. Really, she'd come because Dad wouldn't relent. And yes, she expected to have to forgive Bryce at some point, but not today. She wanted to choose the time, preferably when he was contrite. When he begged her on his knees.

Like that would ever happen.

She dashed the tears from her eyes, hoping no one noticed, but of course Lacey was right there beside her.

"You okay, Mads?" Lacey's voice was low.

Madison shook her head quickly. She wasn't okay. Not even a little bit.

"He seems to be trying."

"Yeah, he does." Her voice caught on the admission.

"Hey." Lacey slung her arm over Madison's shoulders. "It's okay to be conflicted."

"I'm not." Madison twitched her sister's arm away.

Lacey chuckled. "Yeah, you are. I can read you like a book, remember? But how about just taking it one day at a time. Get acquainted with each other again and see if it leads anywhere. Either way, he needs to get to know Everly, and she needs to know him."

"I know." That didn't mean God wasn't having to pry her grip off the situation, one clenched finger at a time.

"Want me to ask again about the horses? That might be easier than sitting in a circle in here."

"Sure. Whatever."

"You hate not being in control, don't you?" But Lacey's question was more of a statement.

"You think?"

"Oh, sis. It will all work out. It will. We're all praying for the three of you to figure it out."

Was there something to figure out? She wasn't sure. Gah, Lacey was right. Madison vastly preferred taking charge. That had all slid to the wayside when she'd welcomed Bryce's advances. Look where that had gotten her.

She glanced to where Everly stood a few feet away from Bryce, eyeing him. Bryce smiled at his daughter but was smart enough not to reach out.

"Horses sound like a good idea," she whispered to Lacey.

"Are you afraid she'll go to him voluntarily?"

Everly wasn't generally a shy child. It wouldn't be the first time she'd met a stranger who didn't stay one, but that was always within her familiar sphere at home. Not like this.

"Maybe I am afraid of that. I've never had to share her before."

Lacey elbowed her. "Hey."

"You know what I mean. You guys and Dad and Nancy are family."

"Bryce isn't a threat, Mads. Look at him."

Madison didn't need to be told. She could hardly tear her gaze away from him except for her daughter. Their daughter. She bit her lip as the two eyed each other. Then she stepped forward and clapped her hands. "A trip to the stables sounds like a great idea. Can you make it happen, Bryce?"

CHAPTER FOURTEEN

"Hey." Weston led Jamie's pony, Sparkles, into the corral as Bryce and company arrived.

"Thanks, man." Bryce glanced around. "Want me to take it from here, or do you want to?"

Weston shrugged. "You'll be fine." He rubbed Sparkles' jaw as he handed the halter to Bryce. "I'll be inside." He disappeared into the shadowed interior of the stables.

That guy never much liked people. Bryce shouldn't be surprised he'd handed responsibility over. On the other hand, Weston trusted Bryce, so that was good, right?

Bryce turned to Madison's family. Mila climbed on the rails to see over. "A pony! Can I ride him?"

"You kids may take turns. This is, uh, Sparkles."

"Sparkles?" Madison's eyebrows shot up. She and her sister exchanged grins.

"You heard me. He's Jamie's pony. I think the moral of the story is to never let a toddler name an animal."

"Aw, it's a cute name." Lacey stepped up beside her daughter. "And he's a cute pony, right, Mila?"

The little girl nodded, eyes shining. "He's beautiful."

Bryce wouldn't go quite that far, but whatever. "So, uh, one person can help Mila, but everyone else should stay on the other side of the fence, okay?"

"Sure." Lacey clambered over then lifted her daughter to her hip. "You get to go first."

Bryce would have let Everly go first, but it wasn't likely the toddler cared. A glance toward his daughter — *his daughter!* — in her mother's arms, revealed a wide-eyed child. "Everly's next."

"Mine turn," Griffin insisted.

Rob stepped up beside his son. "You'll have a turn after Everly."

"Mine turn *now*."

"He can go next," Madison said softly. "Everly doesn't care."

Rob shook his head.

"No, really."

Mila tugged at Bryce's shoulder. "Help me?"

"Of course." He lifted her from Lacey's arms. "Swing your leg over the saddle, okay?"

"Like this?" Mila settled on Sparkles' back.

"Perfect. Now hang onto that big bump. It's like a door-knob, right? I'll make sure Sparkles doesn't buck you off."

The little girl giggled. "Okay."

Lacey stepped back as Bryce led Sparkles in two slow circles around the corral. When he stopped the pony, Mila bent and hugged its neck. "I love you, Sparkles. You're so pretty."

"Come here, sweet thing." Lacey reached for Mila. "It's someone else's turn."

"Can I have another turn, Mr. Bryce? Please, please, please?"

"I'm sure you can, after Everly and Griffin." Saying his daughter's name out loud still seemed strange, but getting outside had been a great idea. Now they had something to focus on rather than awkward conversation.

"Take Griffin next." Madison backed away from the corral fence.

"If you're sure." Did she not trust him to be careful? Whatever.

Rob lifted his son to the pony's back. "Hold on tight, okay, buddy?"

Griffin bit his lip. "My's scared."

"I'll walk beside you then. I won't let you fall."

Bryce led the pony at an amble.

"My's gonna fall!"

"No, you're fine, Griff. Daddy's right here. I won't let you fall. Remember how we talked about Jesus always being beside you? He will keep you safe, too."

Bryce nearly tripped over his own two feet at Rob's quiet assurance. The man put a new spin on things. If God were that kind of father, then... yeah, He could be trusted. Dad might not have been attentive, but he wouldn't have let Bryce fall, either. Not on purpose. But God didn't get sidetracked from His job of taking care of people.

Huh. Something to think about when he wasn't responsible for the safety and entertainment of three little kids.

When Griff's ride was done, Bryce turned to Madison. "Ready?" He held out his hands.

Madison looked from his face to his hands to his face

again. She got it. She knew he was asking for more than a pony ride. He was asking for her trust.

It was all for Everly. It wasn't personal between them.

But it could be.

No, she'd never trust him again. Why should she? He'd let her down once, completely.

Could trust be rebuilt? How much did he care?

Time stood still. For how long, Bryce wasn't sure. But then Madison squeezed Everly. "Want a horsey ride, baby girl? Bryce will take you just like Mila and Griffin."

"Horsey!" Everly jumped around in Madison's arms.

Madison held her toward Bryce.

He tucked his hands beneath the toddler's armpits and brought her close to him. He'd held Simon plenty of times. That little guy was chunkier than Everly. Less... delicate.

"Hey, Everly." Bryce barely dared breathe as he took in the beautiful child in his arms, her features so much like her mother's. "Want to sit on Sparkles' back?"

She pointed. "Horsey!"

"Aw, that's cute." Lacey's voice sounded distant. "She doesn't know very many words."

"You can ride the horsey." Bryce carried the precious load over to where the pony stood patiently. He set Everly in the saddle, her short legs horizontal on Sparkles' wide back.

No way was he letting go, and for some reason, Madison hadn't joined him. How was he supposed to lead the pony while holding the child? Not that Everly likely cared whether or not they were in motion.

"I've got it." Rob stood at Sparkles' head and took the

halter. He gave Bryce a knowing nod as though he understood the surge of emotions rocking Bryce's world.

Bryce kept his hands lightly around Everly's middle as they strolled around the corral. He could feel her heartbeat through her snowsuit, feel how fragile her little life was.

Who knew he was capable of these surging emotions? Gone was his usual cynicism. In its place slipped a sense of wonder and awe.

He'd helped to create this little life, but it hadn't just been him and Madison. God was the ultimate Creator, even though the situation had been less than ideal. This beautiful child was the result. Could she be a heavenly messenger to remind him of the bigger picture?

Because... God.

Bryce could barely breathe as awareness of the Almighty engulfed him. He clung to reality, because Everly's safety and Madison's good will depended on that grip.

With a start, he realized the pony was still, and Rob stood beside him. "You okay?"

"Yes. I think so." Bryce turned slightly so his back was to those gathered by the fence. No one needed to see the tears he was blinking back. Dratted emotions, anyway. But were they so terrible? Wasn't this moment worth a little leakage?

"She's something special." Rob jutted his chin toward Everly. "So's her mom. I'm on your side, man, just don't hurt them. Either of them."

Bryce squared his shoulders. "I'll do my best."

And that was something he'd rarely said or done in the past. Just getting by wasn't good enough this time around. Everly deserved better than that. So much better.

"COME TO MAMA, BABY GIRL." Madison hadn't been able to stand it any longer, so she'd climbed over the rails.

Everly's fingers tangled in the pony's mane as she beamed proudly. "Horsey!"

"Yes, that's a horsey. Come?"

Everly patted Sparkles.

Bryce's bare hands still wrapped Everly's torso. Madison had been very familiar with those hands once upon a time. They wore a few more scars than they had two years ago. They were the hands of a working man.

They were attractive.

Bryce was attractive.

He shouldn't be, though.

The scene was like a still photo. No action, just her outstretched reach, Everly's gleeful grin, the pony's back, and Bryce's hands.

Slowly her gaze lifted to his face.

He was watching her, his eyes searching hers. "She likes it." Wonder filled his voice.

"She seems to."

"She belongs here on the ranch."

"What?" Madison reared back, the tableau dissolving. "No. She belongs with me. You promised."

Bryce gave his head a quick shake as though he was trying to make sense of the conversation.

"You said you wouldn't take her away from me. I won't let you!"

"That's not what I said. I mean, that's not what I meant when I said she belonged here. I meant she likes the ranch, and she maybe even likes me a little. I don't want you to take her away from me."

"But…" Her fearful flash faded, and she released a long breath. "We can talk about that later. Right now, I want to spend a bit more time with my family. They're driving back to Jewel Lake right after dinner, then flying home tomorrow."

His hands flexed around Everly, who still patted Sparkles. It was like he couldn't get enough of his daughter.

Madison knew the feeling, but she'd been experiencing it for almost 16 months. For him, it was brand new.

She hated feeling sympathy for him. He'd been such a nitwit. Yeah, she remembered, but that was then, and this was now. Dad had been right. She hated admitting that, too, but facts were facts.

"They'd like to see around the rest of the ranch," she said softly. "And honestly? There's a lot I haven't seen, either. We were all locked up in the lodge half the time I've been here because of that snowstorm."

"Right." Bryce looked thoughtful. "Give me a second, okay?" He lifted Everly off the pony, tucked her into his arms, and strode to the stable door.

"Hey!" But Madison's protest sounded weak even to herself. He wasn't going to steal Everly or hurt her. His action was merely a natural one for a father.

Lacey stepped up beside her. "What's up?"

"I'm not sure I like this."

"Relax."

"Easy for you to say."

Lacey chuckled. "You think so? I might feel a little possessive of your kid, too, you know. But she's fine."

Just then, Weston followed Bryce and Everly out of the stable. "Bryce says you're looking for a ranch tour?"

Madison glanced around her family. "Um, sure?"

Weston thumbed toward Bryce. "He suggested a hayride. I only need a few minutes to hitch Dolly and Cinnamon to the wagon. They'd like a bit of a stretch, I'm sure."

"A... a hayride?" Madison looked between the men.

Bryce was grinning. "Sure, why not? Weston will drive the pair, and the wagon gives us a good space to ride and talk to each other. My truck is too small for all of us."

Everly stretched toward Sparkles. "Horsey!"

"I guess I should unsaddle the pony, as Weston will be busy with the team." But he didn't make a move to pass Everly back to Madison.

"I guess you should, since none of the rest of us knows how." Madison plucked her daughter from Bryce's arms.

He looked bereft, his gaze bouncing between them as his weight shifted from one foot to the other. "Okay." He led Sparkles into the stable.

Madison's breath whooshed out as she pivoted to the railing where her family stood, all wearing wide grins.

"A hayride!" Nancy clapped her gloved hands. "That sounds like a lovely way to tour this ranch."

"It... does." Madison felt the ground quake beneath her. The whole universe seemed to be tilting. Life would never be the same.

Sharing Everly with Bryce would not be the end of the world, after all, but did she need to be the one to make the move across the country? He thought Everly belonged at the ranch, but Jewel Lake wasn't far. Madison could find a little house for the two of them, and Bryce could take Everly on his days off. Right? There was no need for Madison to stay at Sweet River. Her job could be done anywhere with good internet. But, wow, she was going to miss Dad and Nancy and Lacey's family.

She took a deep breath. That was tomorrow's problem.

In minutes, they were seated on the wagon while Weston drove the horses.

"This is Hummingbird Lane, where much of the staff lives." Bryce pointed out the duplexes. "Grandfather and Maxwell are talking about something more like an apartment building over there. We have a lot more staff than the original owners anticipated."

Dad engaged him in some chat about staffing needs as the wagon trundled on.

"This is Dragonfly Lane. These cottages are rented out by the night or week. They're usually full from Memorial Day until well into fall. We've got two other groups of cottages, as well." Bryce pointed through the trees. "The road to Eagles Nest Lane isn't plowed because there's nothing much there yet, but we'll be putting in eight treehouses there this summer. That's my brother Maxwell's next big project."

"Treehouses!" Lacey elbowed Rob. "We need to come back and stay in one of those when they're ready!"

Bryce looked at Madison so long she thought he'd never look away. "My brother has a lot of good ideas."

"You do, too," she breathed.

"I'm not smart like Max or a leader like Tate."

"You're you, with your own talents. I've seen photos of the grounds on social media. It looks very inviting."

He seemed taken aback. "Really?"

"Yeah. Really."

The wagon rolled back to the other side of the lake. Bryce looked around. "This is the RV park. It's been pretty popular over the summer, too."

"There's a playground, Mommy!" Mila pointed. "Can we play?"

"Do we have time?" Lacey asked.

Madison checked her watch. "For five minutes or so, if Weston doesn't mind. Then we should head back to the lodge."

Weston shrugged. "Take your time. I've got nowhere else to be."

CHAPTER FIFTEEN

T hanks."

Madison shifted away from Bryce as they watched her family drive away in the rental van, honking and waving. This was too final. Also, Bryce stood too close. She glanced up at him. "Thanks for what?"

"I know I crashed your family time. Thanks for being gracious about it."

"It worked out."

"Buh-bye." Everly kept waving from Madison's arms as the taillights faded.

"You *were* planning on introducing me to them, right?"

She cringed at the censure in his voice. The shiver that ran through her wasn't only because of the chilly night as they stood on the covered deck. "At dinner?"

"In front of everyone."

"Um... yes?" Okay, that might not have been her finest idea.

"Why?"

Madison swallowed hard. "Because I'm a coward, I guess."

"Buh-bye?" Everly peered into her eyes.

"You and I are staying here for a while, baby girl."

Everly's lip began to quiver.

"Look, I need to settle her for bedtime." Madison turned toward the door.

Bryce's warm hand touched her forearm. "Wait. Were you afraid of me?"

"You haven't given me much reason to trust you."

"I'd never hurt you."

Madison studied his face. "But you did. Physical pain is only one kind. Repeated rejection does a number on a person, too, you know."

He looked down. "I treated you terribly. I was a block-head. I'm sorry."

"You didn't know... but you also didn't give me a chance to explain."

Everly snuggled into Madison's shoulder and tucked her thumb into her mouth.

Bryce's hand hovered like he wanted to touch Everly, but he withdrew and shoved his hands in his pockets as though to keep them out of trouble. "Madison? We can go over this a thousand times, and the outcome will be the same every single time. I was a horrible person. I get it. I'm sincerely sorry. Can we move forward from that?"

She hadn't expected him to be so blunt about it, but that was the crux, wasn't it? She had to let it go and let bygones be bygone.

"For Everly's sake," he added.

For Everly's sake.

Madison would do a lot for her daughter, including attempting reconciliation with Bryce. But she'd never expected a contrite Bryce. She'd expected him to either sue her for custody or laugh her off. Either way, she'd figured she'd be headed back to Pittsburgh within a few weeks at the most.

Now?

Now she had no idea.

"Madison? You're scaring me."

Bryce had shifted closer again. She could smell his cologne mixed with horses and hay. She could feel his breath on her cheek. It would be far too easy to lean into his once-familiar embrace.

"That's why I'm still here, Bryce. To try to move forward."

"What do you mean, try? We *are* moving forward, so long as we keep talking to each other."

"I said I'm trying. I meant that."

"Okay." He huffed out a foggy breath. "I thought Christians were supposed to forgive. I don't think that means saying the words and then clinging to a grudge."

"I'm not doing that."

One eyebrow tipped up. "Sounds like it to me."

"Shows what you know," she muttered. He'd hit the nail on the head, though. What did forgiveness really mean? The old mantra was to forgive and forget. But forgetting was a bad idea. It left a person wide open to the same thing happening to them again.

The Bible also talked about forgiving someone seventy times seven. That was a whole lot of mercy. More than Madison was capable of.

But not more than God was capable of.

"We need to have some family dates. Can we start tomorrow?" Bryce's eyes looked tortured. "I know she's not ready to spend time alone with me. She needs to know me a little first, so you get to put up with me, too."

"Are you asking me or telling me?"

"Telling you, since you don't seem to be open to asking."

Nail, meet head.

What he was proposing was reasonable. He was right that she couldn't let him take Everly on his own yet. He was right that he should get to know their daughter. He was right that Madison needed to be present.

That didn't mean she had to like it.

It didn't mean she should feel that little tingle of anticipation for these family dates he spoke of. All too soon, he and Everly would be comfortable with each other, and Madison would no longer be needed.

There was nothing between her and Bryce anymore besides their child. She didn't want there to be. Okay, fine, she possibly did. She'd obviously not learned a thing two years ago to still be attracted to playing with fire. She was smarter than this. She could be near Bryce and not succumb to his charm. She could. She had to.

BRYCE STOOD outside in the cold long after Madison had retreated indoors with a drowsy toddler nestled on her shoulder.

He'd scored a major victory, but it seemed hollow.

Two weeks ago, he'd have told anyone who asked that

he was lucky to be rid of clingy, needy Madison Woodrow. The absolute gall of her to follow him to Montana two years after he'd broken up with her!

Okay, a tiny bit of him had been flattered, but more of him had been wary. Nutcases like her sometimes needed a restraining order to keep a decent distance.

He'd never dreamed the secret she'd been trying to share with him, and he'd been too full of himself to hear a word she said. Now, she'd given her all to set him straight.

Footsteps crunched on the snow, breaking the silence.

Bryce looked up the lane to see Graham and Cadence approaching hand-in-hand. A shaft of envy pierced him. Graham was such an unassuming, nerdy, numbers guy — though he preferred the term *geeky* — and here he was with a gorgeous wife who clearly adored him.

No one would ever have called Bryce unassuming. He'd been brash, cocky, mean, even. He was not a nice guy, and he didn't know how to change that.

He'd never wanted to be a nice guy before now. Not until reality had smacked him across the head with a two-by-eight.

Was it too late to change his ways? It felt like it. Madison clearly thought so, or she'd give him the benefit of the doubt.

"Hi, Bryce," Graham said as they mounted the steps.

"Hey."

"How did it go with Madison's family? We were praying for all of you."

Oof. Bryce so did not deserve that. "Uh… not as bad as I was dreading."

Cadence kissed Graham's cheek. "I'll just be inside,

honey." She gave Bryce a quick smile and entered the lodge, light and laughter spilling from indoors for a moment while the door was open.

Then it was dark and silent again, but his cousin stood beside him, hands in his parka pockets, his breath puffing in the frigid air.

"I'm fine. You don't need to hang out with me."

"I want to."

Alrighty, then. When had Bryce ever been this selfless? He couldn't remember a time. "Okay. Thanks."

"Want to talk about it?"

His default flippant response nearly popped out, but Bryce managed to hold it back. These guys all managed to talk to each other without sarcasm or bravado, even Weston, lately. Maybe they knew something Bryce didn't.

He scoffed lightly under his breath, a puff of vapor crystallizing in the cold. They definitely knew something he didn't. For the first time in his life, he wanted to be part of that club. To have actual friends among his brothers and cousins and others, not just people required to put up with him because of genetics.

"She didn't want me there," he blurted. Then winced.

Graham nodded but said nothing.

"Paisley told me they were in the activities room, so I invited myself."

"How did it go?"

Bryce mulled that for a moment. "Madison's niece wanted to see the horses, so we went over to the stable, and Weston helped me get Sparkles saddled up for the kids. I put Everly on the pony."

Graham searched Bryce's face. "How was that?"

"Truth? Amazing. She's so tiny. So fragile. So... alive." Her heartbeats beneath his hands were a sensation he'd remember forever as the moment he'd begun to fall in love with her.

"That's the first time you touched her?"

"Yeah." And he was itching for more. Tomorrow? "Weston took us on a sleigh ride around the ranch so they could see the beauty all around here. See my home."

"Your home?" Graham's eyebrows peaked.

That was something else Bryce had never expected, to become at home in rural Montana. He shook his head and grinned at his cousin. "Weird, huh? But yeah, this is home. At first, it was only a place where Madison couldn't find me, even though I'd finally blocked her number. I was so dumb."

"I didn't want to be here at first, either, but Grandfather didn't leave much room for our opinions."

"Truth." Stars pierced the velvety blackness above the trees like so many diamonds. "Yet here we are."

"What are you going to do about Madison and Everly?"

"I'm going to date them."

"Madison is open to that?"

"Not really, but she understands that I need to get to know my daughter and she needs to be present until Everly is comfortable with me. Ergo, family dates."

"Interesting motivation for dating."

"I don't deserve anything more than that."

Graham angled toward him. "How so?"

"I mean, I know I wrecked any possibility of Madison ever fully trusting me again. I can't hope for that as a resolution. All I need is a small piece of my daughter's life. I don't even deserve that much."

My daughter. Those words kept coming out of his mouth. When would they feel real?

"There are a lot of things in life we don't deserve, but God still loves to give us extravagant gifts."

Bryce huffed a laugh. "I think the Almighty looks at me a lot like Madison does. I had all the chances any guy could possibly need, and I blew them all. I'm on my own now." He froze. He hadn't meant to spill his thoughts on religion to anyone at all, let alone Graham.

"I've learned there are a couple of things we need to look at clearly, objectively. One is ourselves. Looks like you are seeing yourself clearly. I have plenty of critical faults. Just because they're different than yours doesn't mean they don't exist."

"Fair." A guy couldn't argue with that. "And the second thing?"

"We need to see God clearly. He's not like us. He doesn't view us like we think He does. He loves us, plain and simple."

The truth jabbed at Bryce. "How can we understand something that's foreign to us?"

"I don't know that we truly can." Graham stared up at the night sky, chewing on his lip. "But we don't have to understand things to believe them."

"This from Mr. Number Cruncher."

Graham chuckled. "I hate to admit it, but not everything lines up in tidy columns. God is wilder than that. Freer. More vibrant. He doesn't color within the lines we've set for Him."

A tiny crack formed in Bryce's life view, and brilliant, pulsating color burst in. Could Graham be right? Was there more to life than the boxes Bryce had laid out to contain the various aspects of it? Madison hadn't stayed in her box. Bryce was peering over the edges of his own.

And God? There was no box that could begin to contain Him. No matter what understanding Bryce was capable of, God was vaster by far.

Humbling.

It was also an unsettling emotion and thought. Bryce liked being in control. He didn't like imagining a power that couldn't be imagined. Whatever postage-stamp-sized impression he could come up with couldn't compare to the Creator of the universe Who'd spoken all life into being.

He'd spoken Bryce Daniel Sullivan into being.

He'd spoken Everly Louise Woodrow into being. God could easily have prevented her conception, but He hadn't. He wanted her.

He wanted Bryce.

Bryce cleared his throat, trying to dislodge the accumulating emotion. "I'm not sure what to do about that."

"About God being so much vaster than we can imagine?"

"That... and everything else."

"Ask Him. He'll show you."

Was it really that simple?

But... what if he didn't like what God revealed?

CHAPTER SIXTEEN

Madison resisted the nearly overwhelming urge to beg Bryce for information on what he had in mind for tonight, but a girl had to have some pride. It wasn't like this was a romantic date, but who knew the definition of a family date, anyway?

The lodge had been quiet all morning while everyone was in town for church. She'd skipped. If she were going to stick around, she'd need to find a church home. Everyone at the ranch seemed to attend Creekside Fellowship, but an online search revealed a couple of other churches that might suffice. Places she wouldn't have to run into Bryce every Sunday morning.

She fingered her phone while Everly napped. She'd been pretty sure Bryce had blocked her two years ago, though there was no way to know for sure without flat-out asking him.

So, she'd retaliated in kind when she'd given up on him and moved to Pittsburgh. Not that he would ever notice or care, but it had still felt defiant.

Now? They would need to communicate about Everly. Keeping him blocked seemed petty under the circumstances. Did he still have his old number? She'd retained hers, so it seemed at least a 50-50 proposition that he had, as well.

Nothing ventured; nothing gained.

Madison poked through her phone settings to unblock his number. It figured that the last few visible texts were her increasingly desperate attempts to get his attention from two years back.

Had he removed the block on hers? An online search revealed that communication didn't show until both parties had removed the obstruction.

I unblocked your number, just so you know.

In case he'd done the same. If not, the text would float into the ether.

Madison couldn't remember the lodge this quiet in the two weeks she'd been in Montana. Last weekend the roads had still been blocked, and no one had driven to town for church. She'd heard rumors that many ate Sunday lunch at the diner, though Eryn had left soup and sandwich fixings in the cooler, and Madison had helped herself.

When Everly woke from her nap, Madison changed her, carried her downstairs, and set her by the toybox while she foraged for a snack for them both.

"Voom!"

Madison glanced through the doorways as the toddler picked up a little red car. Hmm. Canned peaches and cubed cheese would make a fine snack. She placed the items on the highchair tray and went to get her daughter.

The lodge doors opened wide, and a middle-aged couple bustled in on a quick blast of chilly air.

The man helped the woman with her coat as they got down to jeans and sweatshirts. Then the woman seemed to notice Madison. Her gaze brightened. "Hi there! You must be Madison. I'm Walter's daughter, Nadine, and this is my husband, Keith."

The man beamed.

Ah, the newlyweds... and they'd heard of her. "Yes, I'm Madison, and this is my daughter, Everly. I've heard about you, too."

"I'm sure you have." Nadine laughed. "Thanks for stepping in and helping Eryn in my absence. It sounds like everything went well, all things considered."

All things included a few days of no power, but yeah. They'd managed. "It worked out."

"And this is your little beauty." Nadine reached for Everly.

Before Madison could explain how shy Everly was with strangers and how unsettled her life had been lately, her daughter leaned toward Nadine.

"Aw, you sweet thing." Nadine gave a twirl, and Everly giggled.

Madison blinked.

Keith grinned and made faces at Everly. She beamed at him, too.

Wow. Their grandchildren must love them... but then Madison remembered who their kids were. Weston was Nadine's son — so was Jude, whom she hadn't met yet — and he was engaged to Paisley with a spring wedding on the horizon. And Keith's daughter was Eryn, who was engaged to Maxwell. No grandkids, as of yet.

"She just woke up from her nap, and I was getting her a snack."

"Mm, sounds good." Nadine tucked Everly to her hip and headed toward the dining hall. "I'll put on a pot of tea for the adults, and we'll visit."

"There are cookies, too."

"Excellent. Cookies make everything better, right, munchkin?" Nadine tucked Everly into the highchair and clicked the tray into place. "Yum. Nice snack. Can you say thank you to Mommy?"

Everly grinned between Madison and Nadine and slapped the tray.

Madison had never felt so unneeded. Or so bemused at someone taking over and Everly letting them.

"She's a force." Keith's gaze followed his retreating wife. "I can't believe I was lucky enough to marry her."

"The word is blessed, Keith Ralston!" Nadine tossed over her shoulder as she filled the kettle. "And that makes two of us."

Madison glanced at her daughter, who was chasing a slippery piece of canned peach around her tray. "I'll get the cookies."

"I hear Bryce was unaware he had a daughter." Nadine set the kettle on the range.

Madison stiffened. She was so over this conversation with everyone.

"Just as my father was completely oblivious to my existence. I'm glad you made sure Bryce knew. It's rough being the kid who doesn't know anything about her dad, not even his name."

"I'm sure your mother did what she thought was best at the time."

Nadine harrumphed. "She did what was easiest for her. Although it takes some talent to pretend there is no elephant in the room."

In the dining hall, Keith sat beside Everly, entertaining her with baby talk.

Madison turned to Nadine. "Unlike your mother, I tried to tell Bryce repeatedly for several months. Also, times are different now. Maybe you need to forgive your mother for her choice."

Nadine's eyebrows shot up as she stared at Madison. Then she shook her head with a grin. "Wow, you don't pull punches."

Had she been too blunt? It wasn't like she had that sort of relationship with this woman. She'd heard bits of her story, but they'd only just met. "I'm sorry."

"Don't be. You're right, not that I love it. My mom has been very annoyed with me for the past couple of years since I began searching the DNA sites and found the proof I needed to meet my father."

"I met your mom. She seems nice."

"She is nice." Nadine blew out a breath. "But I'm not sure she's forgiven me. She's holding my dad at arm's length, too. I think my half-brother has been feeding her doubts about him. Reggie is jealous of all things Sullivan."

"He's probably afraid of losing his mom, like it means his own father has been forgotten."

Nadine looked pensive. "You may be right. That won't

be an issue for Everly, though. You haven't married anyone else or birthed other children, right?"

Now who was being blunt? Madison took a step back. "No. Not yet, anyway." But whenever she tried to envision her future wedding, the groom turned out to be Bryce. So not helpful.

"You two can fix things now. Best case scenario for everyone."

"Best case?" Madison nearly choked on the words. "I don't think so. Having a child together is a poor foundation for a relationship."

"Ah, you're not completely wrong, but you're also not completely right." Nadine wagged a finger. "God can redeem any person, any situation. I think you should give Bryce your best shot before you give him up as a lost cause. Who knows what God can do if you don't give Him the chance to act?"

Part of her yearned for that, but being a single mother had pulled the wool away from her eyes. She couldn't afford to let her guard down now. "I don't think so."

And then she heard a noise behind her and saw Bryce standing beside Everly's highchair, staring at her from narrowed eyes.

What good was unblocking his phone number if she kept her heart locked away?

Self-preservation.

So, what if Madison didn't want him around? She could

just figure out how to deal with it, because Bryce wasn't going anywhere.

Hadn't there been something about forgiveness in this morning's sermon? Fat chance. There wasn't going to be any of that nonsense anytime soon. Not from either of them, it looked like.

"Say, Bryce, I hear I have you to thank for pitching in with feeding the cattle while we were away. You had quite a storm."

He forced his red-tinted gaze to Keith, sitting beside Everly's highchair. Time to calm down. No one needed to hear his current thoughts spill over, especially his daughter. She might be too little to remember, but Bryce wasn't so sure. Memories of his parents arguing were among his earliest.

"It was my pleasure." And maybe his voice was a little clipped now. It wasn't Keith's fault. None of it was, not even remotely.

None of the women's conversation had been meant for Bryce to hear, even though they visited in a public place. Well, he'd overheard it, anyway. How was he going to handle a family date when Madison wasn't even open to the option of anything real?

He'd never come from behind before. Sullivans had the easy track. Money and good looks had paved his way his entire life. It definitely hadn't been his charm, but his friends overlooked the lack of it on account of his true assets.

Which, it turned out, weren't real, after all. Being a nice person went much further, but it was too late for that, at least with Madison. She knew him at his worst, and she was determined to keep him there.

Could he blame her?

Not really, but she was supposed to be a Christian.

So was he, not that he'd ever acted like it, and she was brand-new to the faith. He couldn't expect perfection from her, and he was obviously incapable of it himself.

That's why Jesus came.

The thought arrowed into his heart. Not a new revelation, by any means, but it felt fresh at a time like this. Had he ever really considered it before?

"Have a seat, son. Nadine's making tea."

Bryce glanced over to Madison, who'd turned to put cookies on a plate. If those were her lemon cranberry cookies, he was all in. At least, if she didn't punt him to the door with a well-aimed kick to the backside.

"Don't mind if I do." Stiffly, Bryce lowered himself to the chair beside his daughter. "Hey, little girl. You like cheese? So does your dad."

She held a slobber-covered cube his way with a toothy grin then took a bite, kicking her little legs.

This child right here was the one and only reason he needed to stick it out in Madison's life. Sooner or later, she'd come around, right? At least enough to be civil? He'd had glimpses of that already, though she'd quickly corrected back to her hostile default every time.

Bryce looked past Everly to Keith. "So, how was Hawaii?"

The older man grinned. "Best ever."

What had Bryce expected? The guy was besotted over his bride. Maybe someday Bryce would have that goofy look on his face, too. His brothers all wore it, and Bryce had jeered.

Now he envied them.

How the mighty had fallen. As if he'd ever been mighty anywhere but in his own head. Man, he was a mess.

"Hi, Bryce!" Nadine set a tray with four mugs of tea on the table and slid into the chair next to Keith. "That's sure a charming daughter you've got there."

He felt his chest puff with pride, but he knew better. "That's all Madison's doing. She's a great mom." The words nearly choked him.

Madison set the plate of cookies in the middle and helped herself to one of the mugs, which she doctored with honey and cream before sitting beside Nadine... a long way from Bryce at the large table. She didn't acknowledge his words in any way, shape, or form.

Fine, then. He couldn't expect instant results, though he'd welcome them.

"She must be," Nadine said warmly. "Everly is such a sweetheart." She made baby noises to the toddler, who giggled.

Madison had a sip of tea before looking over the rim at Bryce. "What do I need to know about tonight?"

Surprises would be such a bad idea right now. She needed to know she could trust him. "We're going over to Tate and Stephanie's for dinner so Everly can get to know her cousins."

Madison's eyebrows tipped up.

"Her *other* cousins," Bryce amended hastily. "She knows your sister's kids. Now it's time for her to know my brother's boys."

"Oh, what a great idea!" Nadine looked between them. "They're such a lovely little family, and Everly isn't much older than Simon."

Bryce had to hand it to the woman, but she might be trying too hard to get Madison on the same page as him.

Madison turned to Nadine. "She's six months older. That's a lot at this age."

"True. Simon isn't even walking yet, so my bet is on Everly trying to keep up with Jamie. They'll be so sweet together. Have a cookie?" Nadine held out the plate.

"Thank you." Bryce glanced at his daughter. "Is she allowed one?" he asked Madison. In his world, kids should always be allowed cookies and candy, but this was Madison's world, and he'd do well to remember it.

Madison bit her lip. "She's eaten most of the rest? You can give her about a third of one."

Score one for Bryce! "You've got it." He broke a cookie in pieces and offered a chunk to Everly, who grabbed at it immediately. "Say thank you."

She looked at him with wide eyes as she stuffed the sweet into her mouth.

"She doesn't have many words yet." Madison glared at him.

"It doesn't hurt for her to hear the expectations for later," Nadine said smoothly. "You never know when 'tanku' will be her next word."

Exactly. But Bryce resisted the urge to shove Madison's nose in it.

He was going to learn a whole lot of self-control over the next while. And it would be worth it.

Hopefully.

CHAPTER SEVENTEEN

She's the sweetest little thing. I was hoping for a daughter." Stephanie watched the children play in the other room where the guys sat. "Instead, I got Simon."

"He's adorable, too."

"He is, but he's no dainty little girl."

Truer words had never been spoken. Simon was a solid little guy. "He'll get leaner when he starts walking and running everywhere."

"That won't be for a while. He's only just crawling at nine months."

"Everly was walking at ten."

Stephanie turned wide eyes at Madison. "You're kidding."

"Nope. She was so busy."

"Wow, I hope not for Simon. He's enough trouble as it is, quite honestly. There's not much he can't get into when he puts his mind to it. Plus, he's so quiet that it's usually Jamie tattling on him."

"People always say, 'oh, just wait until he or she is walking!' as though there's something magical about the trouble they can find then." Madison shook her head. "What extra trouble? A crawling baby who can pull to standing and climb up on things can reach everything. There's no extra trouble to be found crossing the open middle of a space."

"Oh, that's so true." Stephanie smiled at her. "I can see I have much to learn from you. Jamie was 18 months old when I met him and Tate, so I know more about the terrible twos than I wish I did, but not as much about babies."

"Jamie seems super well adjusted. You've done a good job."

"Tate was doing amazing when we met, but he was working long hours for his grandfather here at Sweet River and needed a nanny." Stephanie shrugged. "I'd done a ton of babysitting and teaching Sunday school with preschoolers, and I needed a change from my bank teller job in the worst way, so I begged Tate to hire me for Jamie."

Madison grinned. "Never expecting to marry Tate and become Jamie's mama."

"Wrong. That was totally my game plan from the beginning."

"You're kidding me, right?"

"Not at all. Tate Sullivan was a catch, and I don't mean because of the family fortunes. He was sweet and kind and just the kind of man I'd been looking for. I'd have been crazy to let him slip past me."

"Huh." Madison leaned back. Imagine knowing who you wanted and then simply pursuing him. "It's probably none of my business, but any regrets?"

"If you're asking me if we've had any rough times over the past couple of years, yes, we have. I had loads of insecurities I needed to work through, even after we were married. I was sure Tate would tire of needy me. He was so patient."

Sounded like a reversal of her situation with Bryce. He was the immature, needy one, no matter how he liked to place Madison in that role. But was she being unfair? From his point of view, she really had been pushy. With good reasons, but he'd managed not to hear those.

"Now, you and Bryce…"

Best to nip that in the bud. "There is no me and Bryce."

"Right." Stephanie's eyebrows tipped up over an amused grin. "And you believe that?"

"Why wouldn't I? It's true. Yes, we were an item a couple of years ago. Yes, I gave birth to his child. But in the present, there is no 'us'."

"It's not Everly whom Bryce watches all the time."

"Oh, but it is. I've seen him myself, looking at her in wonder." And then steeling her heart against the pull of emotion.

"He watches you more than he watches her. He knows you're a package."

"Look, here's the deal. The last thing I want is a pity relationship where he only puts up with me to access my daughter."

"Oh, sweetie." Stephanie's voice lowered as she touched Madison's arm. "Is that what you think is happening? Why don't you let your preconceptions go and see what God is doing in this moment? You might just be surprised by the real deal."

Madison shook her head quickly. "I don't think so."

"You're proving my point. Release it. Trust God."

She could see what it might look like to Stephanie. It even kind of looked like that to herself. But how could she let go? "Remember the Bible says not to be unequally yoked." Ugh, she hated herself for even saying that out loud, let alone so primly, as though she had it all together.

There was that social media meme that said something like: Not only do I not have my ducks in a row, I don't even know where they are, and that one over there seems to be a pigeon.

Which about summed up Madison's life.

But it shouldn't be her motto. Shouldn't that be, 'judge not, that you be not judged'?

"That's where prayer comes in," Stephanie was saying. "I am not God, and I can't read people's hearts, but it looks to me like Bryce's heart is softer than it's ever been since I've known him. He seemed to be listening intently this morning in church, not zoning out and having a nap as usual."

Ouch.

Madison had chosen not to attend, stating that Everly's life had been upended enough over the past couple of weeks. She wasn't completely wrong about that, but it had been an excuse. She could see it clearly now.

"Give him a chance. Keep praying. Keep moving forward. We're all there with you."

Just what Madison needed was to provide a ringside seat to all of Bryce's family. Maybe she should offer popcorn for the show.

Her conscience stabbed yet again. How could she break

the habit of distrust? Yes, she was here. Yes, she'd broken the news to Bryce, but she still held back. She was never going to throw herself at any man, especially not Bryce. That might have been Stephanie's way, but it certainly wasn't Madison's. She had too much pride.

Too. Much. Pride.

"Look." Stephanie's voice was a whisper and her touch on Madison's arm gentle as she motioned toward the other room.

Bryce sat on the floor, building a tower of blocks, or at least he would be building one, if only Simon didn't knock them over as soon as there were two or three in a stack. Everly picked the blocks up off the floor, handed them to Bryce, and he placed them on top, where Simon knocked them over. Over and over, like a perpetual motion machine.

Was she like Simon, intent on knocking over the blocks before they could become anything at all? And there were Bryce and Everly, focused on rebuilding.

Tears stung her eyes.

Madison needed to change. Needed to trust.

But how?

BRYCE CHUCKLED. Whoever thought kids had no attention span had not witnessed something like this. Simon never tired of tumbling the tower, and Everly never tired of handing Bryce the blocks to rebuild. Bryce just did his part, placing the cubes over and over.

Jamie stood watching them, hands on his little hips. "What you doing?"

"I'm not sure, buddy. Entertaining the babies, I guess."

"Evly not a baby."

"Hmm. Why do you think?"

"Evly walks. Simon crawls."

From his spot on the other side of the rug, Tate snickered. "He's got you there."

Bryce grinned at his brother. When had the air between them ever been this companionable? He couldn't remember. They'd gone into Tate's office for a few minutes after dinner to discuss the finer points of Madison's situation and employment. She probably wouldn't thank Bryce for interfering, but he had to make sure she and their daughter — especially their daughter — were being taken care of.

The women sat by the table in the kitchen, chatting, often glancing this way.

If only Bryce could be a fly on the wall and overhear. Scratch that. He'd heard enough of Madison telling his aunt she wasn't about to give Bryce a chance. Would Stephanie give the same advice as Nadine, or would she tell Madison to run for the hills?

God knew he'd spent his entire life messing up over and over, but that didn't mean he couldn't change. Fact: he *was* changing. This little girl had done a fine job of jolting him out of his perpetual rut and making him realize there was more to life.

He was even talking to God, sort of. More than he ever had before. He'd actually listened in church. He might go to the men's study on Monday. What more did he need to do to prove to Madison he was worth taking a chance on?

Because it wasn't only his daughter he wanted in his life, it was also his daughter's mother. She'd been just as fun-loving… okay, rebellious… as he'd been back in Chicago, but he'd been drawn to more than that. There was something softer, gentler, about her, but also fierce loyalty. He'd seen her inability to give up on him as a negative, but it hadn't been.

Jamie began snatching the blocks and putting them in the basket. Simon crawled over and dumped them back out. Everly's mouth quivered as tears came to her eyes.

"Hey, Everly," Bryce said softly. "It's okay. We can play with something else."

She turned to him with pretty green eyes so much like her mama's. "Pway."

Bryce stretched behind him to the boys' bookcase and snagged the first book his fingers touched. "Here. Want a story?"

"Buk?"

"Yes, a storybook." He held it out, and she came closer. A second later she settled on his thigh and leaned back against his chest with her thumb in her mouth.

Bryce nearly forgot to breathe as he inhaled the baby powder scent of his tiny daughter. Her soft curls brushed his arm, and her chubby fingers reached for the book.

He closed his eyes. She'd come to him of her own accord. Weston would say kids were just like horses. You needed to just sit in their space and be still and win their trust a little at a time. Sometimes it was mutual. Hadn't Eryn spent hours in the stable with Echo? Both of them had benefited.

"Buk?"

Bryce focused on the board book in his hands. It was called *Noisy Tractors*, and it had a button. He pushed it, setting off a little whirring motor sound.

Everly clapped her hands and giggled.

He pressed it again to the same result.

It didn't contain a story at all, just a few blocky paintings of different colored tractors doing different sorts of jobs. It was all way over her head, but the button wasn't, and it showed on every page.

She poked at it with a tiny forefinger, but not with enough pressure to trigger the motor. He held her finger and helped her push harder.

He could spend a lifetime doing this, helping her, sharing her contagious joy. He looked up to see Madison watching him from her seat at the kitchen table. Was that longing crossing her face?

Longing for what? She must have had plenty of moments like this with Everly over the past year and more.

Longing for Bryce? Couldn't be. That went against everything she'd said to him in the past two weeks. Against everything he'd overheard her say to Nadine and others.

She'd been quick and definite in her refusal to entertain the thought of anything further between them, but he could scarcely blame her. He'd been a Class A jerk in years gone by. He hadn't been much better when she first arrived.

Bryce cringed. He'd accused her of being after his family's money. She'd denied it vehemently, but he'd been so sure that was the only reason she could possibly have come.

Now, he'd just spent half an hour with Tate starting the

wheels turning to make sure she and Everly had all the benefits they needed — regular employee benefits and more. And he'd questioned Tate if she truly needed to work in the kitchen. After all, Stephanie had been paid a fine wage to care for a Sullivan grandchild. Why should someone else be expected to care for Everly while Madison did a job anyone could be hired to do?

Would she mind that he interfered? With any luck, she wouldn't figure it out. Hopefully, she'd assume that Tate thought of it all by himself.

Was it just him, or was it awkward in here? Everly still sat nestled in his lap, jabbing tirelessly at the unresponsive button. He looked beyond to the women.

"Come join us?" he asked.

They exchanged a look he couldn't read — which was pretty much any female glance — and came into the living room. Stephanie slipped into the space between Tate's knees where he sat on the floor, and Tate wrapped both arms around her and nuzzled her neck as she leaned into him.

Bryce averted his gaze, but then it immediately tangled with Madison's. What was she really thinking? Because no matter what her words said, over and over, her wistful expression told him a different story.

A story he was beginning to dream toward himself.

CHAPTER EIGHTEEN

L et me carry her."

The baby carrier was already over Madison's head, though she had yet to finish buckling it. She stared at Bryce in Stephanie and Tate's mudroom.

"Please."

Wasn't it enough that Bryce had stuffed Everly in her snowsuit, tickling her until she giggled and squirmed? Did he want to do everything for her?

And there was that predictable shaft of guilt. She couldn't have it both ways. Either Bryce became a responsible parent, or he remained a terrible person. Did she prefer him that way? Or she could be looking for any excuse to cut him back out of Everly's life, with proof he wasn't worthy of parenting.

Slowly she pulled the carrier back over her head and handed it to him. "You'll have to lengthen the straps."

"Okay." He turned the device every which way, obviously puzzled.

Madison crossed her arms and waited.

He sighed. "Help me, please?"

"This way." She hooked it over his head then adjusted the bands to his longer torso and thicker parka. She was much too close. Not only could she smell the unique scent of him but also feel the heat of his body. To say nothing of the heat of his gaze. She stayed focused on the job until she could safely step backward and look at him. "I'll lift her in it."

"I can—"

But she'd already picked Everly up and begun to slip her into the seat facing Bryce.

Bryce caught Everly under the arms and helped steady her as Madison drew the wiggly little legs through. "You do this by yourself?"

Madison arched a look at him. "That and everything else."

"Ouch." Bryce winced.

"I'm sorry." She sighed. "It's just… hard."

"Thanks for coming over!" Stephanie said brightly.

Tate followed with, "Have a nice walk back to the lodge!"

Right. And here Madison had nearly unburdened herself in front of an audience. She managed a smile toward their hosts who stood with their arms wrapped around each other's waists. "Thanks for having us."

"No problem. We were glad to get to know you and Everly better."

"And to see Bryce all googly-eyed over a baby," Tate joked.

"She's not a baby!" Madison protested just as Bryce said, "I was *not* googly eyed."

They looked at each other then Bryce laughed. "Okay, maybe a little." He flexed his shoulders to settle the carrier better. "Ready for the elements?"

"Sure." Madison stepped out into the chilly night where a half-moon hung in the crystal-clear air. She heard Bryce close the door behind them. It was less than a half-mile walk back to the lodge. Earlier, Bryce had deemed it better to walk than to drive. That, right there, was different than Chicago Bryce, who wouldn't have walked more than half a block if he could have taken his sports car. He didn't even have that anymore, having traded it in for a pickup.

"What will it take, Madison?" he asked quietly.

She jolted out of her reverie. "What do you mean?" Oh, she knew.

"You've been sending mixed signals for two weeks now. You are here. You told me Everly is my daughter. So, thank you for that beginning. But after that, I'm at a loss."

"Oh?" The lodge was much too far away. On the other hand, now was probably a good time for this discussion.

"I feel like you want me to fail."

Oof. How had she been so transparent?

"And your silence tells me I nailed it. But why?"

Oh, Lord, please help us get this conversation right. Whatever right is.

"You're correct that I didn't trust you."

In her peripheral vision, she saw him nod. "I understand that, two weeks ago. I'd done nothing to prove I'd changed since Chicago."

"Uh huh."

"Your revelation caught me flat-footed. I've had a lot of time to think since you let me in on your secret. It was like a two-by-eight to my head, making me see how selfish I've been. I know I'm not going to be perfect from here on out, but please, can't you see that I'm trying? I really want to step up and be the guy you need. The father Everly needs."

"What did you say?" she breathed.

Bryce turned to her. "Quite a lot. What part are you asking about?"

"You care about me? After all that?"

"Yes. Is that so hard to comprehend?"

"Wow, way to romance a girl."

He winced. "I get it. I have to show you, not just tell you. But yes, Madison, I feel like we have another chance to get it right. And we really can't afford to get it wrong, for our daughter's sake."

"That doesn't necessarily mean getting together again."

"No. You're right." He looked up at the sky, and she could see the moonlight reflected on his pensive face. "But my feelings for you have never gone completely away, no matter how I tried to convince myself, you, and everyone else otherwise. I'm no Casanova. I know I'm too quick with sharp remarks instead of mushy stuff, but I'm honestly going to try my best."

Madison's thoughts whirled. Was this the declaration she'd been looking for? Did she really want to open herself back up to being hurt by Bryce all over again? He was no sweet talker. Hadn't been two years ago, either, but he'd demonstrated his affection other ways.

Physically. Sexually.

And she wasn't going there again.

"Madison? Talk to me."

She heard the desperation in his voice as she turned

to face him. "I still have major misgivings. But to make sure we're on the same page, I'm not open to a physical relationship again. Been there, done that, got the baby. Next time I have sex with any man, he will be my husband."

"Me, too." He laughed. "I mean, I'll be married to the next woman I have sex with."

"You have a bit of a reputation here at the ranch."

Bryce rolled his eyes. "Everyone likes to gossip. Yeah, I've dated a lot, but I've always kept it light and flirty. I promise you. You're the last."

Did he mean she'd been the last or she would be the last? Best not to ask. He might not know the answer, and she might not be ready to hear it if he did. "What are you asking for then?"

"I want to see where a relationship between you and me might go, not just because of Everly, though, of course, she's in the mix either way. I... I care about you, Madison."

"Why did you break up with me in Chicago?"

"Fear."

She blinked and looked at his moonlit profile. "What?" Not what she'd expected to hear.

"I was afraid of how deep my feelings had gotten for you. I was afraid I'd be no better at a relationship than my father was. It just seemed easier to let you go. Maybe you'd find some guy more worthy, someone who could stick it out for the long haul."

Anger spiked. "You didn't even try."

"You're right." He turned to look at her, his face shrouded in shadows.

But she didn't need to see his eyes to recognize the

remorse in them. It was clear in his words. Where did they go from here? It was up to her.

BRYCE WAITED, feeling all the weight of the universe on his shoulders in this moment. If Madison said no now, it would probably be forever.

Thumb in her mouth, Everly nestled against his chest.

He cupped his hand on the back of her head, fingering the curls that had escaped her knitted hat. This precious human being didn't deserve the drama surrounding her conception and birth. He would do everything within his power to provide her with the security he'd never felt from his own father.

"Okay."

He focused on Madison with a jolt. "You're sure? You'll give me a chance? *Us* a chance?"

She nodded. "I can see it would be best for Everly."

For Everly. "Do you… still… feel anything for me?"

Madison's shoulders shuddered with a big sigh. "More than I wish were true, honestly."

A grin spread across Bryce's face. "I get it. I really do. But you won't be sorry." How could he make sure of that? No idea, but he'd make it happen. Proving himself to Madison was his number one job in life, starting right now.

He wasn't one bit like his father. He'd gone out of his way to demonstrate it his entire life. He had nothing left to prove. He could chart his own course without fear of retracing James Sullivan's footsteps.

"So, can we start dating now?" Bryce held his hand out to her.

Madison huffed a laugh, but she took his hand. "Isn't that what tonight was? A date?"

Thankfully, he hadn't worn gloves, so he could feel the delightful sensation of her palm against his. He squeezed her fingers lightly. "This was a *family* date, which is not the same thing as a *date* date."

"Hmm. How do they differ?"

"That's a great question." He'd never courted a single mother before. Definitely not the mother of his own child. How could they go out without Everly? Should they include her in everything? "I'm open to ideas."

Her fingers tensed in his.

Was he supposed to sound more confident? The old Bryce had a cocky answer for everything. It was going to be an adjustment to think before he spoke. "What sounds like a good date to you? With or without Everly? Jewel Lake has fewer options than Chicago."

"Understatement." But she laughed. "I don't know, Bryce."

"Let's don't overthink it, okay? Time together can be as simple as—" he cast his mind around the days they'd been snowbound "—playing chess by the fireplace. Or going for a horseback ride. Or—"

"Do you ride?"

"I do. And I think Weston would let us take out a couple of horses now that some of the snow has melted and settled. He wasn't too keen on me riding during the storm."

Madison looked at him incredulously. "You wanted to ride *then*?"

"I was, shall we say, extremely frustrated and in need of clearing my head."

"I can see that." She sighed. "I'm sorry—"

Bryce turned, pressed a finger over her lips, and nearly forgot why in the beauty of the instant. "You have apologized and been forgiven. I have apologized and been forgiven... I think."

She nodded.

He yanked his finger away. Too distracting to touch her lips when this was a vital conversation. "So, now we're not going to express old regrets anymore. Next time we apologize, it will be for something new. Okay?"

"Okay."

Now he just needed to make sure he didn't do anything stupid ever again. He didn't have the greatest track record on that score, but hey, a guy could try. Madison and Everly were worth him turning over a new leaf.

Bryce tugged Madison's hand, and they resumed walking toward the lodge. It couldn't be good for Everly to be out in this cold much longer, no matter how bundled up she was.

"I don't know who to trust with Everly if we should go on a date without her."

His heart leaped. "There's no shortage of women around the place. Paisley loves kids and says she wants half a dozen. I'm sure she'd be happy to watch Everly sometimes. Or Eryn or Cadence."

"Asking Paisley is a good idea. She seems really nice. I don't know her as well as Eryn, of course."

Here was his opening. "Do you want to stay working in the kitchen now that Nadine is back?"

Madison shrugged. "It's not perfect, but I don't think there's anything here that's a good match for my skill set."

"You can tell Tate that."

"Right." She huffed. "It's not that I hate it, but I don't know how I'll manage Everly at the same time. She did better at Stephanie and Tate's tonight than I expected, but I'd rather raise her myself. Which sounds selfish and needy."

"How did you manage in Pittsburgh? Your sister?"

"Lacey helped. I took an online course to become a medical transcriptionist when I moved there. It was something I could do from home with a newborn to give us a stable income."

He hated that she'd had to deal with that alone.

"Lacey and Rob had a vacant apartment above their garage they let us live in. It worked out."

"Medical transcription? I don't even know what that is."

"I turn voice recordings into written records for the clinic I work for."

Bryce chuckled. "You are way out of my league, woman. I know how to turn my computer on and off."

"And run landscaping programs, most likely."

"Well, yeah…"

"Which I have no clue about. It's not a competition, Bryce. Lots of different jobs are needed to make the world go 'round."

She was right about that, but Bryce couldn't help but feel he'd settled on labor that didn't require him to strain his brain overly much. He wasn't number-smart like Graham, a born leader like Tate, or master of every tool he'd ever met like Maxwell.

"Bryce? Everyone says the grounds here are stunning in the summertime. If landscaping is what you enjoy, then it's a great career."

He felt a puff of pride. "They do look a whole lot better than when Grandfather bought the place two years ago. Everything was rundown, but you can't imagine how thick the weeds were. It was such a mess."

"And you brought beauty out of chaos."

"Yeah, I guess I did."

Now all he needed to do was bring order out of the chaos he'd caused with Everly's conception. Like the resort grounds, the bones of the beauty were present. It would just take time to tame the weeds.

CHAPTER NINETEEN

Everyone in the lodge's great room stopped talking and swiveled to watch as Madison and Bryce entered from the cold.

Inwardly, Madison cringed. It was difficult enough navigating all this with Bryce without so many avid onlookers. She shed her jacket quickly. "I'll take her from here. It's past her bedtime." Honestly, Everly was totally asleep against her daddy's chest.

Bryce rubbed his daughter's back. "Can I help?" Then he seemed to notice their audience, and his face shuttered. "Maybe another time."

Madison lifted Everly out of the carrier, which was more difficult than getting her in it had been. Bryce had helped then. He'd help now, if she'd let him. And she'd let him, if they weren't making a spectacle of themselves already.

"What, you guys have nothing better to do than stare at us?" Bryce challenged.

"Nope!" Paisley called back. "You're the most entertaining thing that's happened all day."

Bryce plucked the pink knit hat off Everly's head, perched it on his own, and struck a bodybuilder pose.

Madison bit her lip as she tugged Everly's boots off. She should do the rest upstairs, away from prying eyes. They meant well. She knew that, but she and Bryce could do without the ogling. What had she expected? She should be thankful his family and friends were invested in the outcome. They had Bryce's back. They also had hers and Everly's.

That didn't mean she wanted to share the moment with them. This whole thing with Bryce was too new. Madison wasn't entirely sure what she should be thinking would happen next. Had she hoped for a goodnight kiss? No! Not so soon.

Then why did she care if everyone watched? She made no sense, even to herself. Once she hadn't cared who saw her on Bryce's arm, but she also hadn't been concerned about her reputation back then.

Things had changed. Not only was there Everly to think of, but she'd made a stand for Jesus. She didn't want to let Him down, either. Which had what, exactly, to do with being watched?

"Good night, everyone!" Madison tried for a bright tone as she turned away from Bryce, clutching a sleepy toddler, still in her puffy suit, to her chest.

"Hey," Bryce said softly, touching her arm. "Coming back down when she's settled?"

Madison shook her head. "I don't think so. I... need some time to think."

His hand dropped as he searched her gaze. Then he nodded. "Okay. See you tomorrow, then."

"Okay." She hurried up the stairs. Was Bryce going to hang around the group and tell everyone they were dating again, or would he head out, too? People would figure it out, sooner or later. It was likely better to direct the narrative than let them speculate.

Too new. Too fresh.

She laid Everly on the bed and changed her into a clean diaper and a cozy sleeper. Then she held the sleepy toddler close and rocked her, smoothing the tangled curls. "Oh, baby girl. I think your daddy might love you."

She'd never thought Bryce was capable of true love, not even when they'd been together. He'd always held himself somewhat aloof, as though he were somewhat better than others. Now? He'd changed. Maybe he was equal to the task ahead.

The clincher would be his attitude toward God. He'd softened, but was it enough?

Madison carefully laid her precious bundle in the crib and tucked Bunny beside her.

She shouldn't be judging Bryce's spiritual life. She'd skipped church two weeks running. Well, the first time, they'd been snowed in, and Mr. Sullivan had read some scripture while they listened to praise music.

She'd left her guitar in Pittsburgh. Too bad she hadn't brought it. Playing would have helped her sort through her thoughts and feelings. Worship music always did.

Was she staying in Montana? Would she be sending for all her belongings? Aw, man. She would miss Lacey and Rob and the kids. Dad and Nancy.

She curled up in the easy chair and picked up her Bible. Not that she'd been neglecting it, exactly, but there had been so much turmoil in the last while that it'd been hard to settle her spirit.

Now she paged at random. *Lord? I need Your assurance. I need to see Your love.*

Oh, look. Jeremiah. What verse did she know in that book again? Right. 29:11. *"For I know the plans I have for you," declares the Lord, "plans to prosper you and not to harm you, plans to give you hope and a future."*

Hope and a future.

Madison's heart lifted a smidge. God had her best in mind. She kept on reading. *"Then you will call on me and come and pray to me, and I will listen to you. You will seek me and find me when you seek me with all your heart. I will be found by you," declares the Lord.*

Her finger touched the verses, and she read them again. God wanted to be found. If Bryce sought Him — if *she* sought Him — He would be found.

God wasn't out there with His back turned or, even worse, laughing at her predicament. She *knew* that, but she also needed reminders of His love and attention to detail.

A soft tap came on her door. Why couldn't people text instead of knock? It wasn't that hard!

She rose to her feet and glanced in the crib on her way by. Everly was sound asleep, her thumb poised for re-entry should the comfort be needed.

Madison cracked open the door. "Yes?"

"We were just checking to see if you're okay," came Eryn's voice.

Madison pulled it open further to see Kaci beside Eryn.

"I'm fine. Really." But the concern on their faces nearly undid her. "I was just reading my Bible and talking to God."

"The best place to go." Eryn shifted from one foot to the other. "I ignored God's word for too long when I was all hung up in my own problems."

Kaci touched Eryn's arm. "Hey, your sister was killed. That wasn't a minor issue, and you were grieving."

Madison knew for a fact she'd be a total mess if Lacey died, but then they were close, unlike Eryn and her twin had been.

Eryn lifted her chin. "But I should have run to God. Instead, I wallowed. At least Madison has her priorities straight."

Did she, though? Madison turned to Kaci. "Sisters are complicated, I think. Do you have any?"

Kaci bit her lip. "No. Just a couple of brothers."

Eryn turned to Kaci. "You've never told me about your family."

"There's not much to tell."

"Two brothers?" Madison laughed. "You must have a lot of stories."

Kaci shrugged. "I prefer not to talk about it, if that's all right with you."

What if Madison pressed and said it was *not* okay? She caught Eryn's perplexed expression. Should she push? Because now that she thought about it, it seemed like Kaci kept an awful lot tight to her chest.

"Come on downstairs for a while," Eryn said. "We were about to make popcorn."

"I've been out all evening." Madison feigned a yawn. "Besides, I can't leave Everly."

"That's what baby monitors are for, and I know you have one. Bryce is still downstairs, in case it matters."

It mattered, all right. "I don't know..." Madison glanced toward the crib.

"Or just leave the door ajar?" Eryn suggested. "We'll hear her if she cries. It's not like we're being that loud down there."

They hadn't been. When the door had been shut, Madison hadn't heard a thing. But how should she react to Bryce in front of everyone? Was it too soon to let the cat out of the bag? Just because they'd held hands all the way back to the lodge...

It wasn't going to get easier, was it? She sighed. "Okay, just for a little while."

BRYCE HADN'T EXPECTED Eryn and Kaci's mission to be successful, but there she was, coming down the wide stairs behind them. Just a few months ago, Graham had stood only a few inches away from where Bryce sat on the hearth, watching Cadence descend that very staircase in a white gown. Somehow, Bryce's mental banks shifted, and he saw Madison as a bride.

He clutched the edges of the slate that formed the hearth. Way, way too early to be thinking of marriage. On the other hand, wasn't that the end game? It never had been in all the dating he'd done over the years, but now? With Everly in the picture, and a tentative relationship in place with Madison?

His life had tipped once-over-easy in a way that felt like

everything prior had been upside down, and now it had clicked into place in its correct orientation. Right-side up.

Eryn rejoined Maxwell in an easy chair big enough for two, but Madison stood awkwardly at the edge of the group. Her gaze ricocheted off of his. She didn't know what to do right now any more than he did.

But hey, why wait? He tipped his hand slightly in her direction, hopefully an inconspicuous enough gesture that everyone wouldn't jump on it before she could react.

Her eyebrows rose in question.

He nodded. Tried for a welcoming smile. Sure, they had an audience, but didn't this whole crew have their best interests at heart? As hard as Bryce had tried to push everyone away, they hadn't let him but continued to patiently love him. They'd accepted Madison. They adored Everly.

Madison crossed the space in front of the group and sat down beside him on the hearth.

Bryce reached for her cold hand.

"Anything you want to tell us?" Maxwell inquired with a chuckle.

"Yeah, sure." Bryce tried to gain some strength from Madison, but she was looking at the floor. He squeezed her fingers. "We're going to give this our best shot."

"Finally," Maxwell muttered.

"What do you mean, finally?"

"Just what I said. Hey, we're here for you." Maxwell looked around. Graham nodded, and so did Weston. "We'll be praying for you."

"Madison?" Kaci asked. "Is he speaking for both of you?"

Bryce realized Madison had a death grip on his fingers. He covered their joined hands with his other one, pressed his shoulder against hers, and felt her inhale deeply.

"Yes. I can't say I don't have any doubts, but this is why I came."

It was? He turned to her with questions in his eyes.

She nudged him. "I just didn't think there was any universe where it might seem viable."

In other words, she'd expected him to remain an egotistical idiot. Well, he hadn't given her much reason to hope otherwise. "I get it. But it's different now."

"So, uh…" Maxwell cleared his throat. "I'm not saying it's impossible for a leopard to change his spots, but, well, it's nonviable without God. Just sayin'."

"Yeah, about that." Bryce met his brother's gaze. "You still going to that men's study on Monday night? Is it too late to join up?"

Maxwell's eyebrows shot up. "You serious?"

"As serious as a heart attack."

"Let's not wish one of those on anyone," Weston drawled. "But, to answer your question, yes, we're going and, yes, you can come."

"Thanks, man." Bryce managed a grin at his cousin. The guy wasn't so bad, after all. Then he looked at his kid brother. "If it's all right with you, Maxie?"

Maxwell winced. "Do you have to call me that?"

"Only when you're being a pain in the butt."

"Whatever." He shook his head. "We're glad to have you. Pastor Eli is leading, and there's quite a group. You probably know most of them."

Bryce turned to Madison. "That's my next step then. I'm going to prove to you that trusting me isn't a mistake."

Graham cleared his throat. "May I say something about that?"

No one was stopping him. Bryce gestured for him to carry on.

"You're going to mess up again, Bryce."

"Thanks for the vote of confidence." But wasn't that his biggest fear?

"It's human nature." Graham looked from Bryce to Madison then back again. "We can try all we want — and we should try; don't get me wrong — but we're still going to fail. It's what we do with that failure that matters most. We can throw up our hands and say, 'whatever, I tried and failed,' or we can get on our knees, ask forgiveness, and keep getting back in the game."

Bryce stared at him. "Profound, cuz."

"I speak from experience." Graham nudged his glasses back up his nose as Cadence reached for his other hand. "Too many times I just gave up instead of regrouping and starting over with God's help. Man, I don't know how people do life without God."

Bryce knew the answer to that one. "Poorly." He looked around the group. "Anyone else have any words of advice for us at the moment? Might as well get all the barrels at once here."

"No barrels, dude." Maxwell chuckled. "But hey, we could pray. You might have a bumpy road ahead."

Didn't everyone? But Maxwell wasn't wrong.

Bryce's plan was to accept all the guidance as humbly as possible. Even if it went against every fiber of his body.

CHAPTER TWENTY

adison took a deep breath, straightened her top, and tapped on the office door.

"Come on in," Tate called out.

She entered the room, a quick glance revealing Graham frowning at his computer screen in the far corner. Cadence's area was easy to spot with its bright yellow painted desk and bulletin boards covered with neat rows of photos of the ranch and its people and activities. Cadence herself wasn't in.

Madison hadn't paid that much attention that morning two weeks ago, but here she was again, this time facing the acting CEO rather than the owner of Sullivan Enterprises. A lot had changed, but things seemed to be going okay, so why had she been summoned?

"Good morning, Madison." Tate rose from behind his desk. "Please have a seat. I've just got a few things to go over with you this morning."

"Good morning." Madison perched on the edge of the

wooden chair, and he retook his seat. Tate the boss was far more intimidating than Tate, Bryce's brother, who'd hosted their family date last night. "What can I do for you?"

"Well, first of all, the original agreement you made with my grandfather was to work in the kitchen for two weeks while my aunt Nadine was away on her honeymoon."

"Right. And she's back now."

"My grandfather told you you'd have a spot on kitchen staff as long as you wanted it. Eryn will be pouring most of her time and energy into preparing the gift shop for opening later this spring, so we do have that opening."

"Yes." Madison clenched her fingers together. "That is what Mr. Sullivan said."

"That brings up a couple of questions. The first is, are you planning to stay on at Sweet River?"

"I… I'm not sure."

Tate's eyebrows shot up. Across the room, Graham's keyboard stopped clicking. "I thought you and Bryce were giving your relationship a shot?"

"We are. I just don't know if the ranch is the best place for me. I was thinking of finding a place to rent in town for Everly and me."

The man studied her. "You'd need a job in town, wouldn't you? It's a bit far to commute up to Sweet River, though not impossible."

Here went nothing. "I already have a job. I work remotely as a medical transcriptionist."

"So, you've been doing two jobs the past couple of weeks?"

"I took some personal time off."

"I see. That brings me to the second question, then. Do you want to continue in the kitchen?" Tate held up a hand. "Before you answer that, please know we aren't kicking you off the ranch if you say no."

"I'm sure you need the staff housing for paid staff, at least come spring, right? I realize I'm currently in one of the guest rooms, and you'll need that even more for paying guests."

"Here's the thing." Tate folded his hands on his desk and leaned closer. "I'm not sure how much you know of my story with Stephanie."

Madison blinked at the change of topic. "I've heard some?"

"Short version: I had recently become Jamie's guardian. He's the son of my late brother and his wife."

"That I'd heard. I'm sorry for your loss. For Jamie's loss."

"I'm not going to lie. It was a difficult time. Then my grandfather summoned all of us here to the ranch to build it back up and get it in the black. His main motive, however, that we didn't know about beforehand, was to integrate Aunt Nadine, Weston, and Jude into the Sullivan clan as we worked together. Grandfather had recently learned of his daughter's existence."

"Yes, I've heard that story." It too closely mirrored hers.

"Grandfather needed me to jump right in with both feet for 12-plus hours a day, but I had an 18-month-old dependent."

"Enter Stephanie."

"Exactly. But I needed to be near Jamie as well, so

Stephanie moved into the other half of the staff duplex Jamie and I were in. She came on Sweet River payroll as Jamie's nanny." His gaze softened. "It didn't take long for us to realize we were stronger together, but that's another story."

"I'm happy for you." Not sure what it had to do with Madison, but yay.

"What I'm trying to say is this: there's a precedent for a Sullivan grandchild to live at the ranch with a caregiver. In Jamie's case, a nanny. In Everly's case, her mother. Sullivan is happy to offer you a home and a stipend for caring for your daughter here. We will also pick up all insurance costs."

Was this an offer or an insult? Madison glared at Tate, willing herself to stay seated, to remain calm.

"You will always have a home with this family, no matter what happens." He leaned back and smiled.

"I didn't come here asking for help. I was managing just fine on my own."

"We're trying to make it easier for you."

"I don't want an easy button." A slow swirl of panic began to simmer in her gut. "I don't want you involved at all. Everly is *my* daughter, and it was against my better judgment to track Bryce down at all and give him another chance to know he had a child."

Uncertainty flickered in Tate's eyes. "But you and Bryce are trying to make a go of it. At least, that's what the rumor mill says."

Madison gritted her teeth. "It's not ranch business. It's private between us." Yeah, she'd kind of made it ranch business by bearding elderly Mr. Sullivan in his Chicago office.

She'd let him set up a temporary job for her to give her an opportunity to broach the subject to Bryce.

"I understand that."

She pulled to her feet. "Do you? Because my biggest fear coming into this situation to begin with was that Bryce would sue for custody and leave me in the cold. Everly is not a ward of your family the way Jamie was. She's *mine*, and I won't let her be a pawn."

"That's not what I meant." Frowning, Tate leaned back in his chair and studied her. "Not even a little bit. We'd never try to cut you out of Everly's life."

"Then let me handle this my way."

He examined her for another long moment. "What does that look like to you?"

"I think I should move off the ranch. I can't handle having so many people assuming they know what's best for Everly and for me. I don't intend to leave Montana, but I need you all to back off and give Bryce and me space to work this out."

So many people? What of the group of women and their obvious care for her? Eryn, especially, had stepped out of her own comfort zone to become Madison's true friend, truer than any she'd had before. Kaci and Paisley had been right there, too. So had Cadence and Stephanie.

With Lacey clear across the country, didn't Madison need the support of this group of friends? Not if it came wrapped with Sullivan interference, she didn't.

"Hey, Aunt Nadine! Where's Madison?" Bryce had managed to keep from hunting her down all morning, but mostly because he expected to see her in the kitchen when he came in from helping with feeding the cattle.

Nadine looked up with a smile. "I understand her assignment in the kitchen has ended."

Bryce blinked. It had? News to him.

"She met with Tate this morning, and that's all he told me. Eryn is going to stay on in the kitchen part-time for now."

"I... see." He did not see. Why hadn't she let him know? Oh... had he ever unblocked her number? "Thanks." He turned away and checked his phone. Nope, he hadn't. He shook his head and rolled his eyes at himself. *Great way to renew a relationship, moron.*

After clearing the block, he sent her a text. *How are things this morning? I heard you had a meeting with Tate?*

Did he dare put a laughing emoji with that? Maybe not, in light of what Nadine had said. Had Tate made the offer to Madison that they'd planned last night? Probably that was all that was going on, but the thought didn't settle his spirits as it should.

Bryce stared at his phone. Had Everly had a bad night? Or had Madison changed her number when she moved to Pittsburgh? Or... maybe she'd blocked him as well.

He chomped on his lip. He couldn't blame her if she had.

The longer he waited for a reply, the more he had to wonder if something else was going on, but no one had ever called him intuitive. Or tactful. He shoved the phone in his pocket, jogged up the stairs, and tapped on Madison's door. "It's me. Bryce."

You know, the father of your daughter. The guy you are giving another chance.

He'd wrap his arms around her and hug her. Then she'd tell him what was going on, and they'd share their first kiss in over two years.

The door opened with a swish, and Madison stared at him with anger etched on her brow and flashing from her eyes.

Bryce took a step back. "Are you okay? What happened?"

"I'm moving to Jewel Lake as soon as I can get everything packed up." Behind her, those huge suitcases he'd hauled up two weeks ago lay half-filled on her bed.

"I don't understand. I thought we were on the same page on giving us another chance."

"I *am* giving us another chance. From town."

"But... I live here. As do you, right now. What's all this really about?"

"Your brother."

Bryce blinked. "My... brother? Which of them?" Because both were so blasted nice this reaction was laughable. If it had been Bryce, he would have warranted it a thousand times over.

"Tate." Madison crossed her arms over her chest. "I've never been a charity case, and I'm not starting now."

A droplet of a clue began filtering through Bryce's mind. "What, exactly, did he say that got you so riled up?"

"Offering me money to care for my own child! Offering me Sullivan health care and benefits as though he has the right to do it. As though I haven't already handled it all without his interference."

Bryce closed his eyes for a second. Wow, talk about a backfire. "I'm sure he meant well. It does make sense." He watched her nostrils flare. "In a way."

"You knew." Her tone was flat.

"Uh." He scratched his head, stalling for time. But lying was off the table, if he was going to do this relationship right. If she'd even let him, anymore. "Yes? Like I said, it makes sense. You'll have fewer worries and can focus on Everly."

"I don't have any worries." Madison jabbed him in the chest with a fingertip. "None except losing Everly to you and your family. I'm not going to allow it. Do you hear me?"

"I hear you." The idea of kissing her to make her stop these silly accusations and quell her panic flooded his mind, and he eyed her pink lips.

"Do you?" She poked again and whirled away. "No one asked me, just came up with a tidy little package with no loose ends. Well, I need some loose ends. I need to not be wrapped up tight in a spider's web."

Bryce couldn't help it. He laughed. "That's how you see my family? As hungry spiders toying with a captured fly?"

Madison pulled a drawer out of the dresser and tipped it into the suitcase. Her underwear and nighties tumbled in like a colorful waterfall. "I have nothing to say to you right now."

"Madison." He took a deep breath. This was all reversing more quickly than any backpedaling he'd ever seen before. "Can we talk this through rationally?"

"I suppose this was all your idea."

What if it had been? "No one is trying to wrest control of Everly away from you."

"No? Then why did Tate keep talking about hiring a nanny so I could keep working? Why did he insist on paying all these expenses I never asked to have covered?"

"Because he cares about you? Because *I* care about you?"

"We're not there, Bryce. I don't know if I ever can be. I've never felt so, so smothered in my entire life."

"Smothered? You can't have it both ways, Madison. Either you do it all yourself, or you let me in. And my family is part of me." It wouldn't always have been that way, but they'd stuck by Bryce all those years when he was a monumental idiot. He'd stick up for them now.

Even if it cost him losing Madison and Everly? It wouldn't. But what if it did?

"Where's Everly?"

"Paisley has her for a bit." Madison shoved more clothes on top and tried to zip the over-full suitcase.

"Did it occur to you to call me? She's my daughter, not Paisley's. Did it ever occur to you to talk to me about this before reacting?"

"For two seconds, but last I figured out, you'd blocked my number."

"I did, two years ago. But I've unblocked it. I texted you." He pointed at the device plugged in on her nightstand. "As you'd have seen if you hadn't blocked me."

Madison picked it up and turned it over. "Oh."

So, she saw the text preview now. Why hadn't she noticed it ten minutes ago when he'd sent it?

Man, he wanted to shake some sense into her. Or walk away and say he'd been right the first time. She was too dramatic for the likes of him.

But Madison held the key to Everly. Bryce's daughter.

He was going to have to suck it up and make it work.

Somehow.

CHAPTER TWENTY-ONE

I wish you weren't moving off the ranch." Paisley rolled the big suitcases into the hallway. "Where will you stay?"

"At the hotel until I find a rental." Madison settled Everly on her hip and glanced around the gorgeous room she'd called home for two weeks. Too bad it all ended this way, but she hadn't really expected a better outcome.

"That'll be pricey."

Madison shrugged. "Small price to pay for freedom." She followed Paisley to an elevator tucked into an alcove she hadn't noticed before.

"I thought you and Bryce were getting back together."

Tears pricked Madison's eyes. "I thought so, too, but I doubt it now."

"I hate to be the one asking." Paisley punched the button for the main floor. "But have you prayed about this? Sought God's wisdom? Placed the situation in His hands?"

The elevator doors closed. "I've prayed."

"Enough?"

"What are you getting at?"

"Running doesn't generally solve anything." Paisley uttered a sardonic chuckle. "Ask me how I know."

"Sometimes running is the perfectly logical choice."

"If God made it clear you should escape, yes."

Madison huffed. "Paisley, I can't do this right now."

"That means this is exactly when you should stop, take a deep breath, and pour it all out to God. Not reciting all the injustices a thousand times, but becoming quiet before Him, truly asking for His will."

"I'll pray again when I'm out of here. I promise." Though, could Madison really trust God? She'd thought He led her here... but that might have just been Dad pushing until she wore down.

"For I know the plans I have for you," declares the Lord, *"plans to prosper you and not to harm you, plans to give you hope and a future."*

Those blasted tears threatened to overflow. God spoke fine words, but things had not worked out. She didn't feel any hope for a future in which she had any choices.

The elevator doors opened at the lobby level to reveal Kaci and Eryn blocking the way with linked arms.

Great. If Paisley hadn't stepped forward to keep the doors from sliding back shut before looking back at her, Madison would have jabbed another button — any button — and willed the doors to close again swiftly.

Now she knew what a caged animal felt like when the gate was open, freedom just about in sight, but the guards stood right there, ready to recapture her.

Really, Madison? That's what you get out of this? They're your friends. *They care about you.*

She took a deep breath as Everly lunged toward Eryn. "Ryn-Ryn!"

"Come here, sweetheart." Eryn plucked Everly from Madison's arms. "You and your mama going for a car ride?"

"Voom."

Eryn squeezed the toddler. "Yes, voom, though I really wish you weren't." Her reproachful gaze caught Madison.

Was this a mistake? It couldn't be. Madison had to get away before she could think clearly. Yes, yes, and to pray.

Then you will call on me and come and pray to me, and I will listen to you. You will seek me and find me when you seek me with all your heart. I will be found by you," declares the Lord.

If she sought God with all her heart, she'd find Him. Finding was one thing, but could she trust Him? And that brought her back to the previous verse about the hope of a future.

She had to trust Him. The only alternative was to reject Him completely and give up the peace and joy and forgiveness she'd known for the past year. No. God was trustworthy. He was. She just needed to get through this dark time.

Her three friends glanced at each other and nodded like they had a secret language. "We're coming with you," Kaci stated.

Madison blinked. "Coming with me where?"

"To see you settled in the hotel room. To help you find a place to live."

"And to pray together." Paisley wheeled the suitcases out into the back hallway behind the gift shop.

"For how long?" Because Madison hadn't planned to rent a suite.

Eryn grinned. "We'll figure it out."

"But you all have jobs to do." Madison pointed at Eryn. "You, especially."

"I already took today off, since Nadine is back."

No doubt thinking Madison would be in the kitchen. Guilt crowded Madison's mind. Ugh, could this get any worse? Was there any teensy, tiny chance she was over-reacting?

She tried to reject the thought, but it danced around like a boxer, planting more hits to her body and mind.

She *was* overreacting.

Maybe.

Okay, almost for sure.

But she still needed to regroup.

Paisley paused at the corner. "Are you coming, or should I haul this back to your room? It's still yours. Housekeeping hasn't been by yet to clean it."

Kaci chuckled. "She's not wrong."

"I'm going." She reached for Everly.

Eryn handed the toddler over. "I'm riding with you."

"And Paisley is riding with me." Kaci jingled her key fob.

"I know some people in town. I'll start looking for a place for you to live." Paisley patted the pocket where her phone resided.

Madison shook her head and followed her friends toward the lobby. "But you guys still think I'm making a mistake."

"It's not irreversible." Kaci donned her coat at the door. "The biggest mistake would be cutting all of us out at the same time, and we're not going to let that happen. You need us."

Truth. Relief flooded Madison's mind that her friends would not let her go. She'd never had any like that before.

Her Chicago crowd had stopped calling just a few days after she moved to Pittsburgh. If she wasn't there, she wasn't fun. If she wasn't fun, she wasn't their friend. They'd moved on without her, never even knowing she was pregnant.

One who has unreliable friends soon comes to ruin, but there is a friend who sticks closer than a brother.

That was in Proverbs somewhere. Lacey had used it to comfort her when she'd mourned the silence of those former companions. It hadn't been much of a comfort, other than it had helped point her to Jesus.

He was the friend that clung close. She could trust Him. She just needed to get away from the swirling voices and emotions for a little.

To get away from Bryce.

She could tell he'd been humoring her. Almost laughing at her anger with his brother. He hadn't been shocked. More likely, he'd known what Tate would say. Maybe he'd even put his brother up to it.

It was such a guy solution, as though money fixed everything. Hello, it did not. She wasn't after a fat bank account. She made a decent income with the clinic. She'd never be wealthy, but she made enough to live independently. Besides, Jewel Lake had to be cheaper than Pittsburgh.

By the time Madison had Everly buckled into the car seat, Eryn was settled into the Jeep's passenger seat.

"Paisley's not the only one who knows people." Eryn latched her seatbelt. "Harper is the youth pastor's wife. I bet she'd know what's available. Or there's Trinity and Dale. He owns a retail store downtown. He must hear things."

Might this all turn out okay after all?

"YOU BUNGLED EVERYTHING." Bryce glared at his brother.

Tate held both hands up in self-defense. "It was your plan."

"How about reading her body language?"

"I don't know her well enough to do that."

"Oh, really?" Bryce slammed his fist against Tate's desk. "I'm guessing the signs were there, and you ignored them."

"I made a solid offer." Tate set his jaw.

"But one she didn't want. You should have shut up part way through and retracted. Listened."

"Seriously? You're coming at *me* with that? That's rich."

Bryce narrowed his gaze. "What do you mean?"

"Oh, come on, Bryce. You can say whatever you want, be as rude as you like, knowing full well you're hurting feelings, but *I'm* the bad guy here for making your girl-friend an offer meant to ease her worries?"

Was Madison even still his girlfriend? That had lasted, what, 12 hours? No longer than 15.

"Look, bro, I'm sorry. But…"

Wasn't there always a but? Bryce raised his eyebrows.

"But I had no idea she'd be that prickly about it. Seemed like an offer from heaven to me. Stephanie would have been all over it."

"Madison is not Stephanie." If Bryce had ever doubted, he did so no longer.

"So I see. But look. The girls went with her to Jewel Lake. They're not letting her go on her own. She's one of us now, whether she likes it or not, and they'll make sure she lands on her feet."

"She took my daughter," Bryce growled.

Tate looked a little more contrite. "I'm sorry."

"I was barely getting any trust out of Everly. Just that little bit last night where she sat on my lap at your place, and I read to her."

"*Noisy Tractors* isn't exactly a reading book."

"That's hardly the point. We had a system going with the blocks, too. Do you have any idea what it's like to remember exactly two times you ever got to touch your 16-month-old kid?"

Tate sighed. "No, I don't."

"And don't even start with how Wally died and never gets to hug Jamie again. That's not the point, either. Life's not fair. I get that. But I was *this* close to starting a relationship with my daughter and her mother."

"Would it help if I phoned Madison and withdrew the offer?"

"How dense can you be?"

"Look, I've said I'm sorry. I mean it. I was blindsided by her response, but it all came down in an instant. Rather than casting blame, how about we look to the future and ask God for the next step?"

"Can God be trusted?"

Tate met his gaze. "He absolutely can."

"Can God intervene and change outcomes?"

"Uh… yes?"

"You don't sound so confident."

"This is what I know. I know God loves us and wants our best. Ever heard of Romans 8:28?"

"Did Sullivan kids go to Sunday school?"

"Did Sullivan kids learn anything there?" Tate shot back. "Let me refresh your memory. It goes like this: 'And we know that in all things God works for the good of those who love him who have been called according to his purpose.' You hear that, bro?"

"Yeah, I hear it, but what does it even mean? How do I know I've been called according to His purpose? And I can't claim to have loved God particularly well, so I don't think this applies to me."

"It's never too late." Tate's countenance softened. "Not until we're dead, at least. But I know you're called."

"Oh?" Bryce's eyebrows shot up. "Do tell me how you know this."

"You wouldn't be here asking about it if you weren't. The Holy Spirit wouldn't be prodding your heart at all if you weren't open to Him."

"That's backward thinking."

"But it isn't. I've got one more verse for you."

Bryce sighed. "Lay it on me."

Tate thumbed into his phone. "It's from Hebrews three, and it goes like this. Sorry, it's more than one verse, but it's one thought. 'See to it, brothers and sisters, that none of you has a sinful, unbelieving heart that turns away from the living God. But encourage one another daily, as long as it is called "Today," so that none of you may be hardened by sin's deceitfulness. We have come to share in Christ, if indeed we hold our original conviction firstly to the end. As has just been said, "Today, if you hear his voice, do not harden your hearts as you did in the rebellion.""

Today, if you hear His voice.

Was that what Bryce was hearing?

He knew it was. He'd been shoving God into a back corner for most of his life, but God kept coming out, kept showing Himself to Bryce, kept poking at his conscience. And Bryce had hardened his heart, over and over *and over,* but it was still 'today.' He still had a chance to turn back.

Bryce eyed his brother for a long moment.

Tate returned the stare. "You know that story about the lost sheep?"

Did Sullivan kids go to Sunday school?

"Mind if I read it?" Tate jabbed at his phone. "It's from Luke 15."

Bryce's eyes refused to roll. Somehow, he actually wanted to hear this never-ending sermon. "Have at it."

"Then Jesus told them this parable: 'Suppose one of you has a hundred sheep and loses one of them. Doesn't he leave the ninety-nine in the open country and go after the lost sheep until he finds it? And when he finds it, he joyfully puts it on his shoulders and goes home. Then he calls his friends and neighbors together and says, "Rejoice with me; I have found my lost sheep." I tell you that in the same way there will be more rejoicing in heaven over one sinner who repents than over ninety-nine righteous persons who do not need to repent.'"

The old Bryce would have laughed at being compared to a lost sheep. He'd been the *black* sheep, and rather proud of it, but he hadn't been lost.

Except he had. Also, blind.

"Thanks, bro." He turned to leave the room. He had so much to think about.

"Bryce?"

"Yeah?"

"I'm still sorry. Know that, but I don't think God is done with you and Madison. Maybe you both need some time to pray and grow."

"Maybe."

CHAPTER TWENTY-TWO

Thankfully, Lacey had left Madison the slumber pod they'd used for Everly at the hotel a few weeks ago. Now Madison tucked her toddler into the cocoon it formed over the pack'n play, creating a comfy cocoon for Everly. With her favorite lullaby medley playing on Madison's tablet nearby, the little one should be able to nap without interference from the chatter.

And chatter there was, with all three friends on their phones, searching for vacant rentals and sharing information back and forth.

"Wait a minute. Didn't Melissa move out of the Smiths' basement suite?" Paisley asked suddenly. "I wonder if they've rented it again yet."

Kaci pursed her lips. "That's worth a shot. Give them a call."

Paisley tapped in a number. A minute later, she shook her head. "Mrs. Smith isn't answering, and I don't think she has a cell."

Madison's eyebrows shot up. "There are still people like that out there?"

"More than you'd think." Kaci laughed. "Paise, try the church office and ask for Pastor Marshall."

"That means getting past Mrs. McDiarmid."

"Aw, she means well. She just tries to protect the pastors' time."

Paisley sighed and tapped again.

This time, Madison could hear the phone ring then a woman's tinny voice. "Good afternoon. You've reached Creekside Fellowship. How may I help you?"

"Hi, Mrs. McDiarmid? It's Paisley Teele. I was wondering if Pastor Marshall is available to take a quick call."

"Is it church business?"

Paisley rolled her eyes, and the others tried to cover up giggles. "I'd really prefer to discuss it with the pastor."

"Oh. I'll check with him."

"She's such a gossip," Kaci whispered very, very quietly.

"She seemed sweet when I met her," Eryn protested, just as quietly.

"Just a sec. You guys are trying to set me up in your pastor's house?"

All three women looked at her. "Do you want a rental, or don't you?" Kaci asked.

"Well, yes, but..." Wouldn't a pastor want to know all the reasons Madison was here on her own with a baby? Wouldn't he... judge her?

"Hi, Pastor Marshall! This is Paisley Teele. Could you tell me if your basement suite is available for rent right now?"

A low voice replied.

"No, not for me. I have a good friend with a toddler who needs a place for a month or two, and your suite came to mind."

The low voice spoke again, but Madison couldn't pick out words.

"Oh! That's great! Four o'clock? I'll tell her. We'll see you then." Paisley made a show of tapping to end the call and dropped the phone to the bed. "There. We can go have a look nicely after Everly's nap. Now, is anyone else hungry? It occurs to me we've missed lunch at the ranch, and I'm starving."

Eryn nodded. "I could do food."

"Takeout from the Golden Grill?" Kaci suggested. "Have you eaten there yet, Madison?"

"No?"

"Oh, you have to go inside sometime, but not today. It's this hilarious little diner with tacky Golden Girls decor but the most amazing food. Here, let me pull up their website menu."

"Tacky, Golden Girls, and an online menu don't seem like they go together in the same sentence."

Eryn giggled. "You'd think. But I met the owners' daughter, Sage, and she's pretty tech savvy. Or, at least, her husband is."

"Jewel Lake isn't *that* backward," Paisley said. "They've done a lot in recent years to increase internet access to attract digital nomads. Or so I've heard."

"Oh, that sounds promising." Madison sighed. "I need a solid, speedy connection to access the clinic's network. It was painfully slow at the ranch."

The women looked at each other.

"Hmm, something to ask Pastor Marshall about then. I don't know if they've prioritized internet at their house, since they're not really into technology."

"Didn't Harper work from that basement suite for a while?" Kaci asked. "If anyone needs a good connection, it would be her."

All these people Madison didn't know. Could she really make Jewel Lake her home? In Pittsburgh, as in Chicago, people didn't really expect to know each other unless they were next-door neighbors. Possibly not even then.

Everyone-knowing-everyone was supposed to be one of the charms of a small town, but it would take some getting used to, especially if they started getting in Madison's business. But wasn't that just a wider example of what these three women were doing for her right now? Eryn, Paisley, and Kaci were definitely in her stuff, and — surprisingly — Madison was mostly okay with it.

In just over two weeks, they were already like family. Lacey would be doing the same thing if she were here.

Lacey. Madison should phone her sister and apprise her of the most recent developments. She hadn't even told her about Sunday evening... was that really only yesterday? How swiftly and suddenly things changed, first one way, then the other. It was enough to make a girl dizzy. Make her panic.

That was her excuse, and she was sticking to it.

And, yes, praying. She almost didn't want to, but that was another benefit of this friend group. They weren't going to let her turn aside without a fight.

"What do you want to order?"

Madison accepted Paisley's extended phone and scrolled the menu. "Um, what's good?"

"Everything." Kaci licked her lips. "I'm getting the Reuben."

"All of their burgers are delicious," put in Eryn.

Paisley nodded. "They're right. It doesn't matter what you order. It's all good. I'm going with fish and chips and a side salad."

"Um." Decisions, decisions. Madison glanced over the menu. "I'll try the Reuben. I can't even remember the last time I had one of those."

"Excellent choice." Paisley's thumbs danced over the tiny screen. "Should be ready for pickup in 20 minutes. Kaci?"

"Yeah, yeah, I'll go get it, only because Madison is needed here, and I have the only other car. Now I know why you rode with me."

"You offered." Paisley batted her eyelashes.

"I wasn't thinking far enough ahead, obviously."

Paisley elbowed Kaci. "Or I could take your car."

"Not on your life."

"I've never driven a Benz."

"Today is not your lucky day."

Benz? Madison studied her friend. She wasn't that up on car manufacturers, but wouldn't Benz be short for Mercedes-Benz, and wasn't that a luxury brand? How did Kaci afford a car like that on a housekeeping salary? None of her business, probably, but it was a little curious.

"Either way, we have time for a prayer circle before one

of us drives downtown." Paisley settled cross-legged on the bed and extended her hands. Kaci and Eryn flanked her. They all looked at Madison.

No matter the challenges, she didn't have to do life alone. She had friends. She had God.

NODDING to these other men on Sunday mornings or on chance encounters at the diner or feed store was one thing. Taking a seat in their circle in the church basement was something else.

Bryce could only hope his awkward smile wasn't a grimace as he looked around. It felt like a grimace. He'd never tried to smile genuinely before.

He'd never attended a men's study before, either.

"Hey, Bryce. Welcome." Ryder Cavanagh nodded in his direction.

"Great to have you," Caleb Grant, one of the worship leaders, agreed.

"Thanks." Bryce managed not to twitch in his seat and looked toward Eli Bryson, the youth pastor. *Start already, man.*

Eli grinned then turned to Caleb. "Let's have our theme song."

Caleb strummed his guitar and launched into "Good, Good Father."

Bryce listened. He'd heard the song before during church, but he'd mostly blocked it out. Now, hearing a dozen men singing it together, the words penetrated.

Was God really a good Father? The lyrics implied — no, stated — that it was simply His nature, that God couldn't be anything *but* good. But the lyrics continued by stating that being loved by that Father was who we were. Who Bryce was. His identity.

He'd never stopped to consider who he was to God. The black sheep, sure. Someone never good enough, obviously. He'd felt that so deeply he'd embraced that identity.

What if it weren't true?

What if God truly, deeply loved him? Not because he was worthy — Bryce knew better — but because that was simply God's nature?

His world flipped upside down. Or, maybe, right-side up. It was disorienting, giddy, like the zipper ride at the fair.

Oh, sure, Sullivan kids went to Sunday school. "Jesus Loves Me" was likely the first song he'd ever learned, but it had been mere words, not something he'd taken to the bank.

Bryce glanced around as Caleb set his guitar back on its stand and Eli opened his Bible. Everyone's gaze was focused on the pastor.

"We've been talking the past few weeks about God's nature as a Father." Eli lifted his Bible and looked at Bryce. "We've talked about how faithful He is, how loving He is. Tonight, let's talk about His inherent goodness. Let's start with, what is 'good?' How do we define it?"

The guys' expressions turned thoughtful.

"The opposite of bad?" Dale Kennedy suggested then laughed. "I don't know. I've got nothing."

"But what does *that* mean? Do we all agree on what is good and bad?"

Bryce settled deeper into his chair. No way was he getting into this discussion.

Maxwell chewed on his lip. "I think we'd agree, for the most part. But the definition is difficult to pin down."

"Let's say there was no God," Eli ventured. "Would there still be right and wrong, good and bad?"

Bryce knew the answer. Even when he'd stuffed God into a corner of his life and barricaded Him into it, he couldn't silence his conscience. Not completely. Good and bad had remained. But... God had still been there. He hadn't been obliterated.

God had never stopped loving Bryce. Had never stopped reaching out.

The thought crashed over him like a rogue ocean wave, but instead of sweeping him out to sea to be dashed upon the rocks, Bryce felt refreshed. Alive. More alive than ever before.

He blinked, and the basement replaced the shore. The guys mulled the topic of good versus bad as though one of them hadn't just had an out-of-body experience.

Bryce knew what that wave was or, at least, what it meant. He'd never been baptized — of course, he hadn't. A guy needed to make a profession of faith for that to happen in Fount of Grace Fellowship in Gilead, Kansas, where he'd grown up. Same had been true in the Chicago megachurch he'd attended just often enough to keep Grandfather off his back. Probably the same at Creekside Fellowship here in Jewel Lake, Montana.

Profession of faith? What even was that? A statement

that he believed in God… in a good, good Father, who was defined by love for His creation. His people. His… Bryce.

Bryce belonged to his Father. Was loved by Him. And like the song said, that logically meant Bryce was defined as loved by God. It's just who he was, plain and simple.

Nothing was plain and simple.

Dad, for instance. James Sullivan was not that kind of father. He might attend church, but his religion wasn't more than skin deep. No deeper than Bryce's had ever been. Bryce might not have wanted to be like his dad, but this was one area he'd mimicked him perfectly.

Ugh.

But just because James Sullivan had put work and money and prestige before God and family didn't mean Bryce had to keep following those footsteps. Grandfather had kept a better balance, though work had consumed him, as well. It had taken Tate to level the situation by insisting on shorter office hours at Sweet River Ranch and increased family time.

Bryce had never once striven to be like his older brother. He cast a sidelong glance at Tate now. His brother's mouth moved. He must be talking to Eli, but Bryce's head was still in its own time zone. Only his body appeared to be anchored in this basement.

Bryce remembered Tate's baptism years ago. Maxwell's, too. Wally's? Not sure. But when he managed to clear his thoughts enough to rejoin the conversation he sensed going on around him, he'd talk to Eli about his own.

Somehow, it seemed like a first step, a visible, necessary step, toward a public announcement that he wanted to be like his Heavenly Father. He was done using James Sullivan as a guide — good or bad — as to what a dad should be like. From now on, he'd take his cue from the One who fully embodied love and goodness.

Only then could he become the dad Everly deserved and needed.

CHAPTER TWENTY-THREE

S he should never have let Bryce know she'd unblocked his number. The guy texted her like 18 times a day. What did he not understand about her feeling smothered? Did he think this was helping?

Madison looked around the low-ceilinged basement suite that looked like it had last been decorated in the 1970s. The cupboards were painted a dull beige, the sofa covered in a tacky, threadbare floral print. It was clean, though, and safe for an inquisitive toddler. Everly even had her own room, a luxury Madison had been missing since coming west.

She'd claimed the kitchen table as her office space, but she sure wished she'd brought her desktop instead of only her laptop, which was limited in processing power.

She should get Lacey to pack up the computer and send it out.

Or... she could go downtown and buy a new one. There was that store Paisley had pointed out on the town square

— Communication Location: Gizmos, Gadgets, and More. It had looked like the only local option for a computer.

"Want to go for a car ride, baby girl?"

"Voom!" Everly plopped to the floor on her diapered bottom and reached for her boots.

Madison needed to deal with the Jeep rental, too. All her decisions had been short-term. She hadn't really expected to stay in Montana.

She should just go home... but she'd promised Bryce. She'd promised her girlfriends.

After three days, it might be time to reply to Bryce's texts. She'd been busy settling in, sure, but it would only take a few seconds to let him know she'd received them and was okay.

Was she okay? That was the million-dollar question. Part of her knew she couldn't stay in limbo forever, while the other part of her — the childish side — simply said, 'watch me.'

She put on her own outerwear, tucked Everly into her parka, and headed outdoors into the bright sunshine.

"Good morning, honey!"

Madison turned and managed a smile at her landlady, who was sweeping a light dusting of snow off the sidewalk.

"Good morning."

"And how's that sweet baby today?" Mrs. Smith cooed as she patted Everly's cheek.

"She's good. I hope her crying doesn't bother you." Not that Everly had done much wailing, but she'd tripped and bonked her head yesterday, and it had taken a bit to settle her.

"No, no. We can barely hear a thing."

If that was meant to be reassuring, it was missing the mark. Madison shifted the squirming child to her other arm.

"We haven't seen her daddy come around for a visit yet."

Madison's half-smile froze. "We're working on things."

"And we're praying for you both." Mrs. Smith squeezed Madison in an all-engulfing cloud of perfume.

"Thanks. I'll talk to you later." Madison pulled out of the woman's embrace and tucked Everly into the car seat. Yikes. She got that Reverend Smith pastored Creekside Fellowship and that she'd be expected to attend there. The couple probably knew the Sullivans fairly well... although not Bryce, most likely. But this part of small-town living she could do without. Her relationship with Bryce wasn't any of Wanda Smith's business.

"Have a lovely outing!" The woman waved cheerfully.

"Thanks." Why was she so bothered by the pastor's wife? Madison grimaced as she turned toward downtown. That suffocating feeling again. Had she really spent so much of her life in impersonal cities where she could select her interaction level? Pick whom she let close?

Paisley and Eryn and Kaci hadn't let her choose. They'd simply enveloped her. She should resent them... but somehow didn't. Why? They weren't a threat.

Bryce was a threat. The Sullivans were a threat. Wanda Smith... how was she a threat? By representing a church body with expectations.

That was it. The girlfriends had no expectations. Everyone else did.

Madison braked for a stop sign and pondered that

thought. Were they right to have expectations? Was she wrong to resist?

She'd been reading in Philippians, and a few verses from the second chapter had nudged her this morning.

Do nothing out of selfish ambition or vain conceit. Rather, in humility value others above yourselves, not looking to your own interests but each of you to the interests of others.

It was biblical to look out for others. It was selfish and conceited to only look out for her own interests. Well, hers and Everly's, but that wasn't enough to remove the selfishness.

She pulled into an angled stall beside the town square. Communication Location could wait a few minutes. Maybe Everly needed a few minutes to toddle around the park.

And Madison needed to get over herself and text Bryce back. She'd been the one to reach out to him in the first place. It wasn't fair to reject his overtures when they'd barely reconnected.

Truth? She was terrified. Terrified of losing Everly, but also? Terrified of losing herself. Bryce was a lot. He'd ruled her life a couple of years ago by simply shining favor and then disfavor upon it.

She had to trust that he'd changed as he said he had. Had to trust the God who'd done the changing. Had to trust that same God to reform her, as well.

Kids slid around on top of the pond in the park, so Madison didn't need to worry about Everly going through a thin veneer of ice. She plopped the toddler down and watched as Everly gathered a heap of snow with mittened hands.

Madison pulled out her phone and scanned Bryce's texts. They'd gone from terse messages on Monday — frustration with her, frustration with Tate— to ponderings on his devotional reading this morning.

She blinked. His what?

It's hard to trust God the Father when my dad has let me down so many times all my life, but I'm starting to separate expectations.

Madison's dad had let her down, too, when he'd left Mom years ago. Lacey had begged to go along, while Madison hadn't wanted anything to do with him. It had taken a decade or two for her to realize the divorce hadn't been about her and that neither parent had been wholly at fault. Also... Dad had fared better over the years than Mom, having found both a new love and a Savior while Mom clung to bitterness.

Madison didn't want to be sour like her mother.

A quick glance showed Everly contentedly rolling in the soft snow, so she turned back to her phone.

I guess that will be tested when I'm in Chicago for the landscaping conference next weekend, since I'll be staying with Dad. Did I tell you I let my condo go when I moved to Montana?

Is there any chance I can see you and Everly before I fly out on Sunday afternoon? Maybe more than once? I miss you both more than I ever dreamed possible.

Sweet words. Words that were a balm to her spirit... but could she trust them?

Fact: Bryce might be new and improved, but he was still human and would likely hurt her again at some point. But wouldn't anyone?

How long could she cocoon herself and her toddler and keep them safe?

Wasn't security in God's hands? She had to trust Him now or recant of ever professing to accept His great gift of salvation. It was all the way, or no way.

Madison scrunched her eyes shut for just a second while she begged God for both comfort and courage. Then she tapped a reply to Bryce.

You're welcome to visit us in town tonight, if you like.

Then she scooped a giggly toddler into her arms. "Time to go buy a computer, baby girl."

SHE'D ANSWERED!

Bryce had only thought he was resigned to pouring out his thoughts in text to an unresponsive Madison, treating this one-sided conversation like a journal no one would read. He'd given her space, just as she'd asked, but that hadn't stopped him from texting her about anything and everything throughout the day.

May I bring takeout around 5:00?

Sounds good! :)

"Hey, dude. First smile I've seen out of you all week."

"Yeah?" Bryce bared his teeth at Tate. "Here's another one."

Tate slugged his arm. "Too much."

"Do you have time this afternoon to go over the land-scaping plans for next summer? I'm trying to get my ideas in place before the conference, while leaving enough room to switch things up if there are great new products."

Tate raised his eyebrows. "You mean for the treehouse area on Eagles Nest Lane?"

"Yes."

"Uh, you know I have every confidence in you, though, right?"

Bryce's grin felt more natural. "Thanks for that. I know I've screwed up plenty of times—"

"We don't need to rehash forgiveness."

"I hear you, but—"

Tate's eyebrows shot up.

"Thanks." Bryce gulped a swallow. Was this adulthood, finally? If so, why had he fought it tooth and nail? It felt kind of good to be on the receiving end of trust. "I'd still like to run things by you, if you have time."

Tate studied him before nodding. "Sure."

"I'm going into town later to see Madison and Everly."

"I'm sorry I botched that."

"What did you say about rehashing forgiveness?"

"Touché." Tate chuckled. "Okay, let's see what you've got so far."

A couple of hours later, Bryce tucked his laptop in his cabin, got cleaned up, and headed to town. He swung by Petals for the bouquet he'd ordered, then by the Golden Grill for takeout. A fancy dinner at the Chuckwagon would have to wait until they were a little more settled... and had a babysitter.

He held the bouquet in one hand and set the bag of food by his boots while he rang the doorbell to the basement suite.

"Oh, hi, Bryce. I was just mentioning to Madison earlier that I hadn't seen you come by all week."

He closed his eyes, prayed for patience, and glanced up at his pastor's wife leaning out the window. "Hello, Mrs. Smith."

'Oh, don't mind me. Enjoy your evening." She backed out of the window just as the door to the suite opened.

"Hi." Madison offered a shy smile. "Oh. Those are pretty."

A suave reply died on his tongue. All he needed was to provide more gossip for Mrs. Smith. After all, he hadn't heard the window latch. "They're for you."

"Thanks." She took them from his hand as he picked the food bag back up and followed her inside.

Bryce wanted to say how nice her place looked, but it looked like his childhood sitcom reruns had exploded inside. He blinked and set the bag on the table.

Everly toddled into the room. "Mamamama."

He couldn't wait to hear "dadadada." He sat on the floor near a basket of toys. "What's this?" He held out a ball to her.

"Bah."

"That's right. A ball." He rolled it toward her, and she squealed with delight as she chased after it.

Madison laughed. "She plays fetch like a puppy. You're not getting out of that anytime soon."

"I don't mind." Bryce accepted the ball from Everly and rolled it again. "Everything she does is new to me."

"I'm sorry…"

He leaned back on his braced hands and looked up at his daughter's beautiful mother. "Tate and I apologized to each other a bunch of times today and then decided it was counterproductive. He's sorry for all the things, like how he bungled the job offer. I'm sorry for all the ways I've screwed up on company time and taken the family for granted my entire life."

"That was a job offer?" Madison asked, a slight edge to her voice.

"Didn't it sound like one?"

"Not really. It sounded like... control."

Bryce studied her. He definitely didn't want to mess things up any more than they already were. She'd barely let him in the door as it was. "It wasn't meant to."

Madison bit her lip as she lifted items out of the takeout bag. She glanced at him with a pensive smile. "I may possibly have overreacted."

Agreeing would be counterproductive. It wasn't like he'd never pushed buttons or assumed the worst. He rolled the ball again for Everly then rose to stand in front of Madison. "We can start over. Again."

"I don't know why believing the best is so hard for me," she whispered.

"I haven't given you a reason to trust. Not until now." He reached for her hands, tugging them away from the bag of French fries. "Meet the new Bryce."

"The new Bryce?"

"Let's call him Bryce 2.0. There are a lot of the same components as the previous version." He caressed her hands. "But the operating system is new and improved. I've been doing some praying. Some rethinking. Some soul-searching, and, well... speaking of trust, I've decided that my family's mess is no reason for me not to trust God to be a much better Father than my dad has been."

Her luminous green eyes searched his face, her lips lightly parted. "This sounds big."

"It is big."

Everly grabbed his pant leg. "Bah! Bah!"

Did he dare? Sure. He'd never backed off a challenge yet. He reached down and lifted his daughter into his arms. "We can play ball again later. Would you like some food now?"

She patted her tummy then stretched for a French fry. "Foo!"

"I'll tuck her in her seat."

"I can." He'd seen Madison do it in the dining hall. He could figure it out.

"Okay." Madison laid out the remainder of the food, setting a few things on the highchair tray. She placed it in front of their daughter when Bryce had her buckled.

Look at him, acting like a real dad. Then he picked up a couple of plates off the drain rack by the sink. He could act like a grownup in more than one way.

And maybe, just maybe, grownups could kiss.

CHAPTER TWENTY-FOUR

C ould she trust Bryce 2.0? That seemed like today's question, and it was a biggie. Sure, she'd told him she was open to reviving their relationship a few days ago, but she'd been ready and waiting for a scrap of evidence it wouldn't work. Those who hunted for trouble were sure to find it.

Bryce couldn't seem to get enough of watching Everly. He handed her the sippy cup and retrieved it countless times. He offered her tidbits from his burger.

And Madison couldn't get enough of watching Bryce watch their daughter.

Trust... did withholding it from Bryce mean she was withholding it from God? Could she claim to have faith in the Lord without following His nudging to forgive Bryce completely, totally?

What was that verse in 1 Corinthians 13... something about love not keeping an account of wrongs done. She doubted it meant putting herself in harm's way over and over from a blind sense of duty, but it did mean she needed to take Bryce at face value. The change in him over the past few weeks was immense.

Too much, too sudden, to be real?

How could she pretend to be the judge of that? When Jesus's love had broken through her stubborn heart last year, the old shackles had fallen away, and everything had looked brand new. Why couldn't the same be true of Bryce?

It could.

Evidence pointed to the fact that it was.

Did she believe God could change people?

Madison surged to her feet, fled into the bathroom, and stared at herself in the mirror.

Do I believe You, God?

What were the choices? Trust Him... and step out in faith. Or backtrack in her life in Christ. She could all but see the crossroads.

"I choose faith." She said it again, out loud, more firmly. "You've got my heart, Jesus. It's Yours to pour out."

She dabbed the moisture from her eyes and headed back to the tiny kitchen.

Bryce looked up, concern in his eyes. "Are you okay?"

"O-tay?" Everly leaned forward and peered at her mama.

Madison's heart overflowed with love for her tiny daughter as she unbuckled the highchair straps. "Mama is okay, sweetheart." She twirled the toddler in a circle and scrunched her so tightly Everly began to squirm before setting her on the floor.

Bryce was right there, standing in front of her, his dark eyes searching hers. "Madison?"

"I forgive you," she whispered. "All of it. Everything. Love holds no records of wrongs done."

"First Corinthians 13," he said softly, reaching for her hands. "I've been to enough weddings to recognize those words."

Weddings. Not soon, but maybe? Wouldn't that be the best thing for all three of them? To be a family who sought to love like Jesus did? Her heart settled. In God's time.

Bryce's hands settled on her hips. "I love you, Madison. I don't deserve you, but I love you."

She pressed her finger to his lips. "We're not talking about deserving anymore. Just like we've stopped apologizing."

He kissed her finger, sending quivers through her body. His gaze consumed her, not in a hungry way but in a gaze of awe.

Madison recognized that expression. She probably wore it herself. She slipped her hands around his neck, fingering the short hair at his nape. "I love you, too."

Slowly, slowly, his head dipped toward hers, questions visible in his eyes. His hands moved around her lower back.

She wanted his kiss more than nearly anything at the moment, so she pulled gently on his neck until their lips met, brushing lightly. And again.

Just when she was ready to go all in, Bryce pulled back and rested his forehead against hers. "Thank you," he whispered.

Little fingers grappled with Madison's leg. "Up!"

Bryce's smile softened even more — how was that even possible? — and he swept another way-too-brief kiss over

Madison's lips before leaning down and scooping Everly into his arms.

Madison wrapped them both in a hug, her head resting on Bryce's chest. He'd buffed some muscles there since Chicago. Landscaping work seemed to agree with him.

Bryce held the both of them close as well. Everly grasped a fistful of Madison's hair, and Bryce disengaged it gently. "Hey, be nice to your mama."

"Mamamama." Everly bobbed then patted Bryce's head.

He laughed. "Can't grab any, huh? Dada's hair is too short."

"Dadadada."

Bryce forgot to breathe. He swayed on his feet, and only Madison's arm around him held him up. Held all three of them up.

He stared into Everly's clear green eyes while she patted both his cheeks as though it were the most natural thing in the world.

"Did she just…" He blinked.

"She did."

Bryce gulped for air. "Wow. Thank You, God."

"Amen." Madison closed the shortest prayer he'd ever prayed.

Could this be Bryce's new reality? Why had he ever mocked his brothers and cousins for finding romance? But it wasn't only love for Madison swelling his heart, but adoration for this little sprite who'd just claimed him as her own.

"Yes, Everly." He cleared the gruffness from his throat again, doubtless not for the last time. "I'm your daddy. Dada. Papa. Whatever you want to call me."

She tilted her head to one side and studied him. "Dadadada."

"Sounds good to me." He pressed a kiss to her soft cheek then nibbled on the spot.

Everly giggled and leaned back so far Bryce had to release Madison to keep their daughter from falling.

He'd fallen, all right. Hook, line, and sinker for both these redheads in his life.

The little one lunged for her mother, and Madison accepted her with a joy-filled smile and a twirl. "Hey, Everly."

Bryce took a step out of the way and collided with the chair he'd been sitting on at the table. The remnants of their meal were getting cold, and he couldn't have eaten another bite right then if it were forced upon him. Who knew that full hearts made for full bellies?

He tucked the half-eaten burgers back in their wrappers then into a plastic bag he found on the counter.

"You don't have to clean up."

"Why not?" He placed the bag into her sparse refrigerator.

"I wasn't expecting you to do that."

"Get used to it." Just because he'd taken everything for granted when they'd been together last time didn't mean he was still that guy. He wasn't, and it was his job to make sure she knew it beyond a shadow of a doubt. He'd demonstrate the change in every way he could find.

"Thanks." Madison smiled at him in wonder before

sitting on the floor by Everly's toys and reaching for a book.

An actual story, albeit simple, but it didn't have a spring-loaded motor sound like *Noisy Tractors*. Bryce was going to need to get his own copy of that board book.

He wiped the table and highchair while Madison pointed out the exploits of a playful puppy to their engaged daughter. Was it his imagination, or was she exceptionally bright? Not that he had anyone to compare her with. He hadn't really known Jamie at this age, and Simon was still months younger.

Bryce set the vase of flowers on the table before joining his family in the living room. Everly tucked her thumb in her mouth and leaned into Madison as she listened to the story. Looked like someone was nearly ready for bed.

And that would leave time for her parents one-on-one. Bryce would need to be careful not to fall into his old patterns. He wanted to prove to Madison — and himself — that he was a new person in Jesus. He was, right?

Yes.

If anyone is in Christ, the new creation has come: The old has gone, the new is here!

Funny how so many verses he'd learned back in Sunday school had never fully left his memory, even though he couldn't remember the reference.

He leaned over and kissed Everly's cheek then stayed right where he was while Madison tucked the sleepyhead in bed. This basement suite had two small bedrooms, so — decor notwithstanding — it was a step up from Madison's room at the lodge. Would she be open to returning to the ranch? He shouldn't push her, but making sure she knew the offer stood was fine.

A few minutes later Madison settled on the floor beside him, leaning against the base of the old floral sofa. He slipped his arm around her shoulders, reveling in the sensation of her nearness. Enjoying the fragrance of her favorite Carolina Herrera scent. Blessed beyond measure by her trust.

Bryce rubbed her shoulder gently. "Have you ever been baptized?"

She looked up at him in surprise. "No. I kept meaning to in Pittsburgh, but never quite got around to it. You?"

"Never." He managed a chuckle. "I'm not much of a liar, no matter all my other vices. So, I didn't want to pretend to be someone I wasn't."

"Probably good, all things considered."

"Yeah... but I want to be now, or soon, anyway."

"You do?"

Ah, he'd caught her by surprise. He was a little in shock, himself, but once the idea had embedded in his mind, he knew it had to be his next step. "I'm going to talk to Eli when I get back from the convention."

"I forgot you were going to Chicago soon."

Bryce swept his fingers through her long hair. "I wish I didn't have to, but it's one of the bigger shows in the trade, and I need to see what's new and improved."

"How long will you be gone?"

"Four or five days. It will seem forever."

Madison nodded against his shoulder. "It will. Sometime I need to go, too, and see my mom, but I think now is too soon."

"Has she met Everly?"

"She flew out for her first birthday, but it wasn't very comfortable. She sniped at Dad and Nancy and grouched at Lacey because her kids call Nancy 'grandma.'"

Bryce had met Kyra Woodrow a few times while he and Madison dated. She'd never been overly friendly, but then again, he hadn't been any mother's dream-come-true for her daughter back then, either. What would she think of him now? Did it matter?

Somehow, it did. If he and Madison were facing the future together, Kyra would be part of that, if only from a distance. Man, he'd messed up so many relationships over the years...

But he wasn't dwelling on that anymore. One by one, as he could, he'd rebuild, but allowing himself to be over-whelmed wouldn't serve anyone.

"You could invite your mom out west sometime."

"I guess I'm afraid she'd stay and then we'd hate each other."

"Hmm. One more thing to pray about."

"Where is Bryce Daniel Sullivan and what have you done with him?"

"Buried him. This is the new version, remember?"

"I like the new version," she whispered.

"Good. Because he's here to stay, and he loves you." Bryce drew her closer and pressed a kiss to her hair.

Nope, that wasn't going to do at all. He shifted Madison onto his lap and cradled her close, much like he'd held Everly earlier, but so much more satisfying. Then he kissed her. Kissed her again. And... he needed to leave before he did something stupid.

Madison seemed to read his mind as she slipped a little further away then nestled her head against his shoulder. "Ground rules," she said in a low voice.

"Agreed." The word came out a little strangled, and he cleared his throat.

A knock came at the door, and he turned to stare at it without moving. Madison did the same. The knock came again.

Madison shook her head with a small smile, went over to the door, and peered through the peephole.

Good. She needed to keep herself safe.

She opened the door wide, and Wanda Smith bustled in, carrying a pan of cinnamon rolls. "I thought you kids might like some dessert. Did I miss the little one?" Mrs. Smith looked around, all innocence.

"Yes, I tucked Everly in a few minutes ago. These look really good, Mrs. Smith. And smell even better."

Was that virtuous expression for real? Or was the pastor's wife keeping an eye on them?

He should probably be thankful if she was. He stayed seated on the floor. "Hi, Mrs. Smith. That was thoughtful of you."

"Oh, it wasn't any trouble at all. I only wanted to be neighborly. So, are you two seeing each other? Rumor has it Bryce is your little girl's father."

Madison gave Bryce a shy smile. "The rumor is true, and yes, we're seeing each other again."

Wanda studied Bryce until he felt like squirming under her knowing eye. "God will redeem what the locusts have eaten."

Madison frowned. "What?"

The pastor's wife turned to her. "Oh, that's from the prophet Joel. Israel had strayed far, far from God, but He promised that if they turned back to Him, He'd redeem the lost years. He promised to be faithful and rebuild their lives."

"Like that verse in Jeremiah," Madison said slowly.

"Twenty-nine-eleven?" Mrs. Smith asked. "'For I know the plans I have for you,' declares the Lord, 'plans to prosper you and not to harm you, plans to give you hope and a future.'"

"That's the one. I keep coming across it, but I hadn't heard that bit from Joel before."

"Now, God does expect us to walk in the newness of the life He's given us." Wanda gave Bryce a significant look. Had she peered in the window and realized the temptations he'd felt? Didn't matter. She wasn't wrong.

Bryce rose to his feet and ambled over. He slipped an arm around Madison and squeezed her to his side. "I should be going. It's a long drive up the mountain."

"Do have a cinnamon roll for the road." Mrs. Smith extended the container toward him.

He knew when he was being dismissed.

CHAPTER TWENTY-FIVE

So, is this a good thing?"

Madison contemplated her sister's question for a long moment. "Yes. Yes, it really is. He's changed, Lacey. More than I ever dreamed possible."

"Is he fooling you?"

"No."

"You said that rather quickly."

Madison shifted the cell phone to her other ear. "I thought you'd be happy for me."

Lacey sighed. "I didn't think this would happen. I'm not ready to let you and Everly out of my life."

"But you agreed with Dad and Nancy. You pushed me to come to Montana and confront Bryce."

"Keyword: confront. I thought it would do your conscience good, would help you say goodbye to the past and step forward into the future God has for you."

"It's done that."

"A future with some *other* man. Some nice guy in Pittsburgh who could love Everly as his own."

"Bryce loves Everly as his own, because she *is* his own."

Lacey sniffled. "I want you to come home, Mads. I miss you. I miss that babyface."

"I miss you, too, sis. I do, and so does Everly. I didn't expect things to turn out like this. The Bryce I knew two years ago would never have stepped up like this. He's going to be baptized, Lacey. I think… I think I will, too."

"Whose idea was that?" Suspicion threaded Lacey's question.

"His. I never brought it up. He's changed, sis. He really, really has."

"I want to be happy for you, but I have concerns. Have you talked to Dad?"

"Not yet. I'm calling him next."

"He'll want you to come home, too."

Madison wasn't so sure. Her dad seemed to be on Team Bryce even when that hadn't been a popular position. According to Lacey, it still wasn't. "Can't you be happy for me?"

"Are you going to marry him?"

"Maybe, hopefully, one day. He hasn't asked me yet, of course. We haven't dated long enough to be in that place." Those months two years ago barely counted. They'd been so physically consumed they hadn't spent time truly getting to know each other on any other levels.

"I hope you're not making a mistake."

Madison stifled her impatience. "Pray for us? Because we do want God's best, most of all." She did, didn't she? Her desire for Bryce came second place to her desire for God. It had taken the better part of two years to get here, but it was real.

"I will." Lacey paused, and Madison could envision her sister chewing on her lip. "I didn't expect to lose you, is all."

"You'll never lose me. Flights aren't that terrible and go both ways."

"It's not the same as you living above our garage."

"I know. Believe me, I know. We managed to stay good friends when I lived in Chicago. This is no different."

"Except you lived here in between. I'm sorry, Mads. I'm trying to be happy for you. I am, but this just isn't what I expected to have happen."

"But it's how God led."

"Did He? Really?"

Madison hated to hang up on her sister, but there wasn't much more she could take of the negativity. "I need to go, Lacey. Everly will be awake any minute, and then we're heading up to the ranch for a visit." Not that she needed to make excuses, and Bryce wasn't even there. He'd left for Chicago this morning.

"Mads? I'm praying for you."

It didn't seem to mean what it used to. "I'm praying for you, too."

"Talk to you later." And the airspace went blank.

With shaking fingers, Madison tapped Dad's number. He answered on the first ring.

"Hey, sunshine! How are my girls?"

"We're good, Dad. I just wanted you to know that Bryce and I had a long talk last night." She would not mention the kisses. "He's going to talk to the pastor about baptism. So am I."

"Hallelujah! Tell us when, and Nancy and I will move heaven and earth to be there."

"Really?" Her heart warmed. "You'd come all this way?"

"Absolutely. Honey, I knew when we left you in Jewel Lake that there was a solid chance you would never return to live in Pittsburgh. While I loved having you nearby and cherished the time we had together, you need to be where God wants you to be, with the man God has placed at your side."

"Did God place him there, Daddy? Or did I just grab onto him myself?" Because that was certainly more what it seemed like to Lacey.

He chuckled. "God's ways are a mystery, honey. God can and does work all things together for our good."

"Romans 8:28."

"That's the one. So, yes, we'll be showing up at your doorstep at least a few times a year. We don't want to miss everything with Everly... or with you."

"You don't think I'm making a big mistake?"

"In getting baptized?" His voice was incredulous.

"No." She chuckled. "With Bryce."

"Keep moving forward. Keep asking God for direction. Then trust the way He leads you. That's all we can do."

"Lacey's not happy." Aargh, she hadn't meant to throw her sister under the bus.

"I know. She was counting on things not working out with Bryce. She was sure he'd continue to prove himself a jerk and you'd be well rid of him. In the beginning, I wasn't so sure, either. When Walter Sullivan and I chatted in December — before I sent you to his office — he mentioned how he thought Bryce was softening toward things of the Lord. Current evidence seems to support that. Go with God, my daughter. He won't lead you astray."

"Thanks, Daddy. As soon as we have a date, I'll let you know."

"You do that, and I'll talk to Lacey. It's not that she doesn't want you to be happy. She just really loved having you nearby and being an indispensable part of Everly's care. She likes to be needed."

"I'll always need her. She's my only sister."

"She'll come around. Keep in touch, sunshine. I love you."

Madison closed down the call and stared at the fake wood-paneled wall across the room. She'd had immeasurable peace before talking to Lacey. Dad's words had repaired much of that, but he was right. It was God's leading she needed to depend on, not her family's. Was it wrong to want them to support her decisions? Of course not. But she couldn't live by Lacey's choices for her.

"Mamamama?"

"Coming, baby girl! Then let's go see your cousins at the ranch, okay?" Bryce wasn't the only reason to visit Sweet River. Madison was due for some girl time.

"DIDN'T I tell you what would happen if you didn't keep your pants zipped?" Dad raised his eyebrows as he looked across the desk at Bryce.

"To be fair, sir, not really. You've barely spoken to me outside of Sullivan board meetings for the past ten years."

"Would you have listened?"

"Probably not," Bryce conceded. "But I don't think that's the point."

Dad leaned back and clasped his hands behind his neck. "This should be good."

"Why did you leave us all those years ago?"

"Leave you? I left your mother."

"And all four of your sons."

"Your mother asked me for more than I could give."

"Time. Attention. Care."

Dad rolled his shoulders. "This business doesn't have room for slackers if we're going to keep Sullivan Hotels at the top."

"You still don't see it?"

"What? Your grandfather needed Theodore and me to be at the top of our game. The only reason your uncle is still married is that Bridget is just as driven as he is. She doesn't nag him, because she's just as busy. She understands his life."

Bryce could argue with that — their son, Graham, presented a different view — but what was the point? "It might not matter if Sullivan is second or even third best."

Dad scoffed. "That's why you'll never be CEO."

"Tate would also disagree with you."

"He's only in charge of that guest ranch side project. There's not a one of you boys with the balls to head up Sullivan after Theodore and me. Not that my father intends to let go anytime in the next five years." He huffed out a breath.

"I'm sure you've heard that you have a 16-month-old granddaughter, Everly. I want you to know that her mother and I are dating, and that I believe we'll be married in the future."

"Good luck."

"Thank you. But we're not counting on luck. We're counting on God to keep us steered in the right direction."

Dad's eyes narrowed. "I go to church."

Bryce nodded. "I know you do, but you've never once sat me down and explained God's love to me. You've never once told me you're praying for me. You've never once given me a reason to think you took faith seriously."

"How dare you judge me?"

"I'm not judging. Those are merely facts. Honestly, Dad? I'm sorry for you. I'm sorry for the little kid I was who only wanted a daddy who loved him." Bryce rose to his feet. "That's the kind of father I want to be for Everly... one who's present. If that means I don't have a long-term position with Sullivan, so be it. I've learned I love landscaping, and there are other companies that will pay me for it."

"Is that some sort of threat? What do you want from me, Bryce?"

"Nothing. Not anymore. We're building something good out at Sweet River, and we — my brothers and I — are over wishing the past was different. I admit I was slow on the draw. Tate and Maxwell showed me the way. But the truth? I'd still like a father-son relationship with you. The ball is in your court." Bryce put his hand on the doorknob and turned back. "I'm flying back to Montana tonight. See you when I see you."

He heard his father sputtering as the door clicked closed behind him. Man, that felt good. He'd kept his cool and, with any luck, had given Dad something to think about. Would he take the challenge? Literally, God only knew.

A few minutes later, Bryce exited Sullivan Tower onto the blustery Chicago street and tipped up the collar of his trench coat. What he wouldn't give for his down parka right now, but midwestern businessmen didn't dress like western cowboys.

He tugged down his fedora as he turned into the wind and nearly stepped right into a fur-clad woman. "Excuse me."

"Is that you, Bryce Sullivan?"

Bryce took a closer look and realized he was nose-to-nose with Madison's mother. "Kyra! It's good to see you."

She sniffled. "I wish I could say the same to you."

What did she know about his current relationship with her daughter? He wasn't sure. "Do you have a few minutes for a cup of coffee? I'd love to catch up with you."

"You've been seeing my daughter."

"I have." Bryce grinned. "And your granddaughter."

She narrowed her eyes. "Your spawn."

"That would be one way to put it." Didn't he deserve that response? He held his smile in place. "Coffee?"

"I'll give you ten minutes of my time."

"Fair enough." He gestured to the café at street level in the Sullivan building. "Would you like a bite of lunch, as well?"

"No, thank you," she said primly.

Bryce was tempted to order a sandwich for himself anyway, but it could wait. He hadn't been hungry before bearding his father in his den. Now he was starving. A moment later he set two coffees on a small table by the window. If he only had ten minutes, he'd better get talking.

He leaned closer to Kyra. "I want you to know I'm sorry

for how I treated your daughter a couple of years ago. I wasn't in a very good place myself, but that's no excuse. Madison deserved better than me."

"She did. I had high hopes for that girl." Mrs. Woodrow sipped her coffee.

"I'm not sure where you stand on matters of faith, but now, looking back, I can see that God had His hands on our lives, even when we weren't acknowledging Him."

She harrumphed. "Mighty handy to think of God that way. I'm pretty sure He doesn't care what we do, one way or another. If He even exists."

"Oh, He exists, all right." Bryce felt like a little kid trying to explain Narnia to a jaded adult. "He's proved that to me time and time again. I was raised in the church, but I guess I don't need to tell you I didn't act like it. I didn't take God personally."

The woman across from him only tipped her eyebrows up. There was a lot of Madison in her mother. A lot of Everly, too.

"I'm thankful Madison and Everly came to Montana. I'm glad she confronted me. I'm glad that God rapped His knuckles on my hard head and said, 'enough, boy.' I'm glad I listened."

Bryce had her attention now. "Madison and I both acknowledge that God has led us back together. I… I just wanted you to know that. I'm hopeful that one day we'll be married, but we do need a bit more time to make sure."

"I should hope so."

To which part? He wasn't about to ask. "I know Madison would love to see you. Why don't you visit us in Montana sometime soon? Don't miss out on too much time with Everly. She's growing so quickly, and she's really something special." Bryce could hear the wonder in his voice when he mentioned his daughter.

"You're not the same as you were."

He laughed. "I'm not. That's mostly Madison's doing… and all of God's."

"It can't be both."

"It can."

CHAPTER TWENTY-SIX

M adison!" Lacey shrieked.

"Lacey!" Madison laughed as she hugged her sister back. "It's so good to see you."

"We wouldn't have missed this for anything. Besides, it's spring break, and Mila has a week off kindergarten. What better place to spend it than Montana?"

"You said it."

Dad leaned in for a hug. "It's good to see you."

Her eyes filled with tears. "I'm glad you're here, Daddy. All of you." She smiled at the rest of the Pittsburgh contingent. Mila and Griffin were crouched on the airport floor talking to Everly in her stroller. "I wish I could offer you beds at my place, but that basement suite isn't big enough."

"The hotel is fine, sunshine. It's just a few blocks away, and I know you'll be busy later in the week with Bryce's cousin's wedding, right? But tomorrow is a special day for you and Bryce, and we're so glad to be here with you both."

Two months had flown by. Two months in which she and Bryce had met regularly with Pastor Eli for baptism classes that had sometimes strayed into other areas of life. They weren't officially premarital counseling, but topics had drifted into that arena from time to time.

"You're here for the whole week, though, right?"

"You betcha," Dad affirmed. "But don't worry about us. Lacey and Rob figure on hitting the slopes for a couple of days, and Nancy and I will be fine poking around town with the kids."

"Thanks. Everyone is coming in over the next few days. Jude — that's Bryce's cousin I haven't met yet — just got his pilot's license and is flying one of the Sullivan planes here via Kansas." She gulped. "I haven't ever met Bryce's mom before, but she's coming for the baptism and staying for the wedding. Bryce's father is bringing Mr. Sullivan and some of the other family members direct from Chicago. They've got it all worked out."

"That's great, sunshine." Dad squeezed her. "Rob, let's go grab the luggage off the carousel. Nancy, want to pick up the rental?"

Nancy stretched with a quick peck to Dad's lips. "You've got it, Allen."

The trio dispersed, and Madison turned to her sister. "Are you okay?"

"Yeah. I'm sorry I freaked out on you a few weeks ago. It turns out—" Lacey turned away from the kids and lowered her voice "—it turns out I'm pregnant. Can I just blame my hormones for everything?"

"Oh, wow!" Madison hugged Lacey tight. "Sure, that excuse works for me. When are you due?"

"Early September. We'll tell Mila and Griffin soon."

"I'm happy for you. And I'm going to miss squishing your new little one."

"It's not too late to change your mind." Lacey chuckled.

Madison grinned. "It kind of is, though. Montana is growing on me."

"You look happy."

"I am." And she was. While she didn't love the basement suite, it was the best place for her and Everly right now, although Tate had told her the other day that they'd boosted internet access at the ranch. It should be ample for her to access the clinic's files without delays or hiccups.

She'd become acquainted with some of the women from church over the winter. She and Bryce had gotten together with the youth pastor, Eli, and his wife, Harper, a few times outside of the counseling sessions. Ryder and Carey Cavanagh had become friends, as well. They were expecting their first baby this summer.

But she'd also kept up with Eryn, Kaci, Paisley, and Cadence. They made sure to include her often as though she still lived at the ranch and encouraged her to move back, but wouldn't all the staff lodging be full over the summer? The season would soon be ramping up.

"We should meet Nancy at the curb," Lacey suggested, reaching for her kids' hands.

"Yep." Madison pushed the stroller toward the glass doors that swept aside on their approach. "Spring is so beautiful here."

"It's not raining, so that's a start."

"It doesn't always rain in Pittsburgh."

"It doesn't?" Lacey tilted her eyebrows up. "Just kidding. Mostly."

"There's still enough snow for skiing here, even though it's March."

"I'd ask if you wanted to come, too, but I guess you'll be busy with the wedding."

"Maybe next winter when you come? Because, yes, I want to be here for Paisley this week. She's made sure to include me in everything the girls are up to at Sweet River. She's so bubbly and outgoing and made me feel right at home from the beginning."

"Everyone needs a friend like that."

Madison grinned. "You're not wrong."

Dad and Rob exited the airport with a trolley loaded with a pile of luggage. It would have been more, but Lacey had shipped most of Madison's personal stuff a few weeks ago. Having her own art and mementoes certainly made the basement suite feel more like home. She'd had Rob strip her old computer and sell it, since the one she'd bought here in January was an upgrade.

A couple of minutes later, Nancy pulled up at the curb with a rental van, and they all made short work of loading the luggage while the bigger kids danced around Everly.

"I'll follow you guys to the hotel, and we can talk more there." Madison leaned over the stroller. "Say bye-bye to your cousins, baby girl. We'll see them again in a few minutes."

"Buh-bye." Grinning, Everly opened and closed her hand a few times. She was a far cry from the clingy child she'd been in January.

"See you in a bit." Madison pushed the stroller toward her vehicle in the parking lot, the spring sunshine warming her face after a long, cold winter. It was good to see her family, but this was where she belonged.

PAISLEY AND STEPHANIE had insisted on keeping Everly and her cousins on Sunday afternoon so Bryce could take Madison and her family horseback riding around the little lake. There was still a lot of snow higher in the mountains which would keep most of the trails closed for a few more weeks, but today was a gorgeous day, and this was a great way to spend it.

Allen kneed his mount closer to Bryce. "I wanted to tell you how much I appreciated hearing your testimony in church this morning."

Bryce gulped. He'd felt so vulnerable... but also, he'd never been one to back down from a challenge. "It was all true. God has redeemed, well, a lot."

"I'm glad you mentioned that verse in Joel two where God says, '*I will repay you for the years the locusts have eaten.*' It was a verse God brought home to me a few years ago when I was hammered with guilt and regrets. Nothing is wasted in God's currency and timing."

"Still seems crazy." Bryce looked sidelong at Madison's father.

Allen laughed. "That's because He's a crazy, reckless God."

"Right." Bryce chuckled. They'd sung "Reckless Love" after the baptism this morning. It had become a favorite of both his and Madison's over the months they'd been digging more deeply into God's character together. "Thanks for showing me what a godly father is like."

Allen sobered. "I don't deserve any praise for that, son. I failed my daughters' mother years ago. Failed them, too."

"As my father did, but you... well, you give me hope for my own dad, I guess. I'd always hoped my parents would reunite one day, but I don't know as that is something I should be praying for anymore. Not when I see how well you and Nancy exemplify a godly marriage." Bryce offered a wry chuckle. "I want to be you when I grow up."

"We'll all pray for your parents. I hadn't met them before this morning."

Dad and Mom had sat at opposite ends of the Sullivan pew during the baptismal service. Seeing his father's gaze trained on him had given Bryce hope that his own testimony would soften Dad's heart and prepare the ground for God's overwhelming, reckless love.

Now, he gulped. "Thanks."

Allen glanced over his shoulder. Behind them, Rob rode beside Nancy, leaving the sisters with each other. "I'm not sure what your timeline is with my daughter."

Bryce's heart stuttered. "I'm not sure, either. When have we given each other enough time? I don't know the answer." All he knew was his brothers had both jumped into engagement so quickly it had made Bryce's head spin.

"You've been praying about it."

It hadn't been a question. Bryce nodded. "I've talked to Eli some."

"The youth pastor? What's his advice?"

"Go with God. But where is God going?"

"Where do you think?"

"I love your daughter, Allen. I love my daughter, too. I can't think of anything I want more than to marry Madison and become a family under one roof."

"Do you want to know what I think?"

"Of course." But Bryce couldn't help shifting in the saddle and staring straight ahead between Kennedy's ears. Was there any chance Allen Woodrow would shoot him down at this stage?

"You've got our blessing, mine and Nancy's. If there's no solid reason to wait, then don't."

Bryce flashed Allen a questioning look. "You don't think it's too soon? We only reconnected ten weeks ago. That seems crazy quick."

"Time has little meaning, son. Remember the day you came into the activities room and crashed our little family get-together?"

Heat flushed Bryce's neck. "Yeah. That might not have been the best thought-out moment... I've had plenty of impulsive moments like that."

Allen chuckled. "If you could only step back and see the Bryce Sullivan from that January day to the Bryce Sullivan of today, I think you'd answer your own question. You've reclaimed your faith—"

"I didn't have any before. Not really."

"Fair," Allen conceded. "You've found salvation and purpose. You've become a new creature in Christ. I've seen similar growth in Madison through our video chats and phone calls. You kids challenged Nancy and me to dig deeper, too, and not ride on the coattails of our faith."

"Wow." Bryce could barely hear his own response, he was so overwhelmed.

"Are you going to be a perfect husband and father? Nope. You're not. But you two are building patterns of taking issues to God in prayer. Keep doing that, and you'll be fine."

Dad had been so far from perfect, but had he screwed up in every possible way? No, he hadn't. He'd kept in touch with his boys, given them every opportunity to succeed in the family business, and even allowed Maxwell to go off on his own for a few years. He'd loudly resented having to fly to Montana so often for board meetings after Grandfather bought Sweet River Ranch — and especially resented flying via Kansas to pick up Mom — but he'd done it. Sometimes it even seemed like he and Mom tolerated each other.

But would they ever reignite the love they'd once had? Probably not… and it wasn't any of Bryce's business. His calling was to be the best he could be for Madison and Everly and any other children that might join their household.

He looked over at Allen. "Thank you, sir. I appreciate your support more than I can tell you."

"Take care of them." The man grinned. "And believe me, Nancy and I are going to be visiting often."

"There will always be a room at the lodge for you."

"Thanks, son. We'll count on it."

Bryce glanced over his shoulder to see Madison's gaze catch on his. His heart was so full he nearly forgot to breathe. How had he made fun of his brothers and cousins for love? How had he not seen what he was missing in his life by pushing God and Madison away?

I will repay you for the years the locusts have eaten.

He couldn't undo the past. Maybe he didn't even want

to. Every step had led him to where he was today, and this place? Was mighty fine indeed.

Bryce grinned at Madison, and she beamed back.

"Go on, son. Ride with her. I'll catch Lacey and give you a few minutes."

Bryce didn't need to be told twice. He reined Kennedy to the side and waited for Madison on Mirage.

Lacey winked and settled Nutmeg in beside her dad, leaving Bryce and Madison to bring up the rear.

"Happy?" Bryce asked.

"*So* happy." The sun gleamed off Madison's red-gold hair. "I can't think how I could be any happier."

No? That sounded like a challenge Bryce was willing to accept. But not today.

CHAPTER TWENTY-SEVEN

Bryce stood on Madison's doorstep, shifting from one foot to the other. He'd rung the bell, but she hadn't answered, and he didn't dare walk right in. He straightened the lapel of his suit jacket, not that it needed it.

What was taking Madison so long? Nancy had taken Everly to the hotel this morning to allow Madison time to prepare. He'd said he'd be here at 12:30. It was 12:40 now.

The window above his head creaked, and Wanda Smith leaned out. "You're taking our girl to that wedding?"

"Yes, ma'am." He'd become accustomed to her claiming Madison as her own. Bryce was pretty sure he and Madison would have stayed on the straight-and-narrow without her landlady's meddling, but hey, he had to respect her for it.

"Marshall and I will be in attendance, though Eli is performing the ceremony."

"I'll see you up there, then." He pressed the doorbell for, what, the fourth time?

"Coming!" Madison called.

Bryce flexed his shoulders and couldn't help grinning.

The door opened, and he forgot to breathe as he took in the vision that was the woman he loved.

"Too much?" Madison twirled.

"No." He cleared his throat. "You look absolutely amazing."

"You're welcome." Lacey, clad in designer jeans and a tailored T-shirt, edged past them. "She's a great canvas to work magic on."

"Thanks, sis." Madison reached to hug her sister, but Lacey stepped back.

"Don't muss up your dress or your hair." Lacey raised her eyebrows at Bryce. "And you, don't make her cry. Mascara is *not* waterproof, no matter what they tell you."

"I'm not planning to make her cry." But he couldn't take his eyes off of Madison.

One bare, freckled shoulder peeked out of her mossy green gown that wrapped around her waist and fell in an uneven hem to her knees. Her hair had been arranged into ringlets and clasped at the back of her head.

Madison was absolutely stunning.

She was his. How had he become so lucky? Not luck. He knew that. It was all God.

"See you two later." Lacey was halfway down the sidewalk. "Don't do anything I wouldn't do, and don't worry about Everly. We'll be fine with her overnight. We'll bring her to church. Bye!"

Bryce stepped inside, just in case Mrs. Smith was still peering out the window. "You're gorgeous, Madison. You always have been, but this dress? Wow."

She stepped closer and tugged at his lapels. "You clean up pretty nice yourself, Bryce Daniel Sullivan."

"I've had a bit of practice with all these family weddings."

"Eryn and Maxwell's is still to come in August."

"Crazy stuff, my baby brother getting married." Man, he just wanted to drop to one knee right here and now and pull the ring box from his pocket, but no. He had a plan, and he was going to stick to it. He cleared his throat. "But first, Weston and Paisley." Bryce rested his hands on Madison's hips. "Ready?"

Her arms slid around his neck. "Not quite. I need a kiss."

"I can oblige." He dipped his head until his lips met hers. He'd meant for a gentle, light brush, but no. That wasn't enough.

Madison crushed her lips to his.

Had Lacey warned about lipstick? Nope. Just mascara. Bryce kissed Madison thoroughly. Maybe he should propose right now. They could have a short engagement and get married maybe next week. He groaned against her mouth.

She kissed him once more then settled back onto her elegant heels. "I love you."

"I love you more."

"Not everything is a competition."

He angled his eyebrows, causing her to laugh. "I'd win."

"Not so sure about that, buster." Madison's hands drifted down to catch his. "I just need my wrap and clutch."

"I just need to catch my breath. You're my undoing, woman."

"Excellent." She winked and sashayed toward her bedroom at the back of the suite.

Bryce kept his polished dress shoes pinned to the tile in front of the door. He'd done little but think about marrying Madison ever since that talk with Allen earlier in the week. Then Bryce had invited Eryn and Lacey to accompany him to a jeweler Eryn knew. The artisan had several stunning rings that might have done, but when Bryce saw the one with two emeralds flanking the diamond, he'd found the one.

Thankfully both women concurred, because they'd have had a hard time talking him into a different choice at that point. Emeralds would always remind him of Madison's eyes... hers and Everly's.

Madison came toward him with a soft cream wrap over her shoulders and a small matching purse tucked under her arm. "I'm ready."

"Me, too." Bryce had never in his life been this ready for what came next... and he wasn't quite thinking of Weston's wedding.

Step by step by step, his future was unfolding, but patience? Had never been his strong suit.

He threaded her free hand around his elbow. "Then your chariot awaits." He led her down the sidewalk to where he'd parked his truck on the curb after running it through the automatic carwash half an hour before. There was enough mud on the ranch road to negate that polished finish before they reached the lodge, but it was the thought that counted.

Bryce handed her up into the cab, waited for her to clear the folds of her dress, then shut the door. As he jogged around the vehicle, he glanced up at the house to see Wanda Smith waving.

He waved back.

THE LODGE great room had been decorated with vast numbers of colorful bouquets from Petals in downtown Jewel Lake. All that color suited Paisley.

Madison clutched Bryce's hand from their seats a few rows from the front and watched in awe as Eryn and Cadence made their way down the sweeping log staircase from the second floor. A quick peek at the guys flanking the fireplace revealed both Maxwell and Graham with stars in their eyes. A moment later Paisley's sister Kait appeared, but Jude's response was bored, if anything.

Madison had only met Weston's brother, Jude, a few days ago. He seemed fairly quiet, but still self-confident. She couldn't imagine how much he'd wanted to become a pilot to endure months away from his home, friends, and family, but he was back at Sweet River now, ready to take tourists sightseeing.

Bryce tugged Madison to standing as the music changed, and Paisley stood tall — and alone — at the top of the stairs in a mermaid-style gown. Madison could only hope her friend had practiced the stairs wearing it.

She glanced at Weston. The guy was wiping tears from his eyes? How could that be from the stoic cowboy? Bryce said she'd seen nothing with Weston since she hadn't known him before Paisley worked her magic on him, but

Madison could hardly imagine him less friendly than he'd been over the past few months.

At the fireplace, Pastor Eli Bryson, not that much older than she and Bryce, launched into the welcome and reason for the gathering.

Bryce slipped his arm around Madison's shoulders, his hand caressing her bare shoulder. She nestled against him and listened to the short sermon and then the vows. Weston's voice rang clear as he pledged to love Paisley for the remainder of their days.

Similarities between Weston and Bryce were sketchy, though they were cousins, but in that moment, Madison could hear Bryce making those same promises to her. Could see the intensity of his gaze and feel the grip of his hands.

She flexed her fingers in her lap and immediately, Bryce's other hand covered hers.

"You okay?" he whispered.

She glanced up at him, his head angled close to hers, his lips inches from her cheek. Was she okay? Sure... but she desperately wanted what Paisley was gaining today: the man of her dreams becoming her husband in front of friends and family. Not Weston, of course.

Bryce Daniel Sullivan was it for her. She'd known that for weeks now. How long was an appropriate time before he'd propose? Although was it so wrong for the woman to do the asking in this day and age?

Somehow, she was still gazing at him, and his eyes were still pinned on hers. He brushed his lips against her cheek then turned to the front again. With full effort, she did the same.

A few minutes later, Eli introduced Mr. and Mrs. Weston Kline, and everyone around them jumped to their feet, whistling, clapping, and hollering.

Madison and Bryce joined them. She was happy for Paisley. She was. But when would it be her turn?

Weston scooped a giggling Paisley into his arms, twirled her around, and carried her to the back of the great room. Eryn beamed at Maxwell as they followed. Their wedding was only a few months away now. Cadence and Graham came next, looking much more settled in their love at the six-month mark from their own vows. Madison had known Cadence peripherally in Chicago, but they'd never hung out one-on-one. She looked so satisfied and content now.

Paisley's sister Kait tucked her hand behind Jude's elbow and beamed up at him. Jude managed a fleeting smile then marched woodenly to the back, staring straight ahead. Kait might be trying the moves on Jude, but he was having none of that nonsense. Paisley had confided to Madison that she hoped Jude and Kaci would stop being only friends and realize they cared about each other in a deeper way.

Madison snuck a peek across the gathering to where Kaci sat with a few women Madison didn't know. Kaci wasn't looking at Jude any more than he was looking at her. Could Paisley be wrong in her assessment?

Around them, others made their way to the back of the room to congratulate the newlyweds. There would be time for that. Madison wanted to stay in the cocoon of Bryce's arm in the lull of the storm for just a little longer.

In the distance, she could hear the caterers moving

around the kitchen. Nadine had begged to cater her son's wedding, but Weston had put his foot down, as had Keith, Nadine's husband. It was her day to enjoy being the mother of the groom.

"Nice wedding," Bryce murmured into Madison's ear.

She shivered at the closeness. "Yes. All those vibrant colors suit Paisley." Every bridesmaid's dress had been a different color, coordinating with the hues of the bouquets.

"What suits *you*?"

Madison turned to Bryce. "What suits me?"

He studied her intently. "Yes. Colors. Styles. You could just do this gown all over again in white."

"Are you…?"

Bryce shifted in his seat and a small green box appeared in his hand. "I'm definitely asking, Madison Louise Woodrow. I love you, and I can't think of anything I want more than for you to be my bride. Will you marry me?"

She stared at the little box, still closed. His fingers still stroked her shoulder lightly, sending another shiver through her. "I thought you'd never ask, Bryce Daniel Sullivan. I would love to marry you."

His mouth descended to hers, and for a long moment, she forgot where they were. Until she remembered. She pulled back, her eyes wide, and gazed into his deep, mysterious orbs.

"I want to be Everly's dad in every way. Not just the guy who impregnated her mother, but the daddy who tucks her in and reads her stories and takes her for ice cream and to her Little League games. I want it all, Madison. I want it with you."

"I want that, too." Her gaze landed back on the still-closed box. "May I see?"

"Sure. I'd open it for you, but then I'd have to stop hugging you. I hope you like it."

Was that a hint of anxiety in his voice?

She reached for the box with trembling fingers and pried it open. A glistening diamond flanked by two emeralds in a silver setting gleamed out at her. Madison gasped and touched the stones reverently. "Oh, Bryce! It's stunning! It's so beautiful."

Her shoulder felt chilled when he removed his hand so he could slip it onto her finger. "It fits perfectly!"

Bryce grinned and nuzzled her ear. "It should. Lacey made sure of that."

Madison pulled back. "You involved my sister?"

"I did. Eryn, as well, since I knew she'd made many local artisan contacts while working on restocking the gift shop. She didn't lead me astray. At least, I don't think so?"

Madison's heart was full as she touched the ring on her finger. "Neither of them steered you wrong. It's amazing. It's gorgeous and unique and I love you so much."

"I love you more." He leaned closer and kissed her.

"Not possible," she murmured against his lips. "Are we going to compete on that forever?"

"It sounds like a plan."

EPILOGUE

Every time Jude Kline turned around, Kait Teele was right there, smiling at him expectantly. Seriously? She seemed to figure that just because the remainder of their siblings' wedding party was paired up, he should be interested in flirting with her.

Not a chance. He could think of ten reasons why not without stopping for air, but only one reason mattered.

She wasn't Kaci Moore.

Six months in Chicago had only made one thing crystal clear in his mind. Okay, two. He was a Montana boy... and he was no longer satisfied being friend-zoned by Kaci.

How had they gotten here, anyway?

He'd been fine with it at first. After all, he'd been new to being a Sullivan, new to being one of the fortunate few with money, new to working on any guest ranch, let alone his grandfather's.

Too many women who worked at Sweet River had sized him up with all that in mind, but Kaci hadn't. She'd been safe to hang out with because she just saw a fairly shy guy as worthy of friendship.

That's still all she saw.

And Jude didn't know how to make her see more.

"No champagne?" Kait's pouting voice came from beside Jude's shoulder.

He automatically shifted away. "Nope. This is a mostly non-drinking family."

"How boring... but maybe you know how to have fun?"

Jude forced a semblance of a smile to his lips. "I'm afraid I don't. I'm all work and no play, as boring as they come." It was a lie. He'd never known the definition of workaholic until he'd met his mother's two half-brothers, James and Theodore. He'd been a guest of theirs at their Chicago club four times over the winter, and they had no other topic of conversation. Even sharing a passion for flying with Uncle James didn't help them connect.

Not that the man wanted to be called 'uncle.' He still resented Jude's mom for tracking down their mutual father and would prefer to ignore the family dynamics, but Grandfather had been present at a couple of those meals and carried the conversation. Mostly about their hotel empire.

Jude couldn't see his 70-something Nana falling for Grandfather all over again, though there they were, chatting with Mom and Keith while Uncle Reggie and Aunt Melinda hovered nearby with Uncle Kenneth and Aunt Lisa. Mom's half-brothers seemed way out of place in the Sweet River lodge, mostly because they looked around furtively as though trying to place dollar signs on everything.

Their company would be preferable to Kait's though. "Excuse me." He made his way through the crowd, Kaci nowhere to be seen. "Nice to see you, Uncle Kenneth, Aunt Lisa. How have things been going for you?

His uncle sized him up. "All right. I hear you've come up in the world." He flapped his arms.

Jude shook his head. "If you mean fulfilling my lifelong dream to be a pilot, yes."

"Nice to have money, huh?"

It was hard to deny, so he just nodded. And decided his relatives weren't an improvement over Kait, after all. He glanced around again. "I'm glad you could make it to the wedding. It means a lot to Mom."

"Right."

Jude stepped around them and made his way back into the great room, where chairs had been cleared aside and a string trio was warming up for the dance. His skin chilled. Dancing? He had no moves. Okay, maybe he had more than his brother, but not by much, and Weston said Paisley had talked him into dance lessons over the winter.

And Jude would be expected to dance with Kait. Only once, that was for sure.

Then his gaze landed on Kaci, straightening bows on vases of psychedelic bouquets. He crossed the room before he lost his nerve. "Hey."

Kaci flashed him a grin. "Hey. Can you believe all these wild colors? Yet they go together."

"Kind of like Paisley herself."

"You said it." Kaci stepped around him to tuck a fern a little deeper into another vase.

"Hey, want to dance tonight?"

She shrugged. "Maybe once. I'll probably head out early, though."

"Wish I could."

"Oh?" Her plucked eyebrows rose. "I thought you were enjoying the maid of honor."

Jude rolled his eyes. "As if."

"Hey, she's not so bad. Give her a chance."

"I don't want to give her a chance."

Kaci poked his ribs before pivoting away again. "You're not getting any younger, Mr. Hot Shot Pilot."

He patted the spot she'd touched. "Neither are you."

"Yeah, but I'm okay with it. Oh, hi, Kait! Were you looking for Jude? He's right here."

As though Kait couldn't see him for herself. She sure wouldn't have sought out Kaci if he hadn't been standing beside her.

Kait's hand wrapped around his elbow for the umpteenth time today. "Sure was, handsome! Looks like it's nearly time for our dance." She eyed Kaci. "The first of many."

"The first of one." Jude resigned himself to an unpleasant half hour. Kait lived in Phoenix and would be returning tomorrow. He could survive a bit longer in her company, long enough to be polite and not make a scene at Weston and Paisley's wedding.

But his gaze followed Kaci as she made her way back toward the kitchen, about as far away from him as she could get.

Huh. He knew where Paisley's sister, whom he'd just met, hailed from, but Kaci? Somewhere in Texas. She rarely said a word about her family or her previous life, unlike Kait, about whom he knew far too much after the past few days.

Not for the first time, he wondered what Kaci Moore was hiding. It likely wasn't any of his business, but what if figuring it out was the key to removing the friend-zone barrier? He'd have to watch, pray, and see.

A NOTE...

Dear Jude,

Good for you, realizing you want more with Kaci than the once-comfy friend zone. You and your friends are just starting to figure out that she's hiding something. I guess the truth will be out sometime soon now, since yours is the next story, and (cough) it has a slightly revealing title.

You've learned all about keeping a calm head under pressure in your flight training. I hate to tell you how handy that's going to come in for you in the coming months.

Your loving author, Valerie

Dear Reader,

I hope you loved Bryce, Madison, and Everly! It was so fun to write a toddler again. Maybe you felt impatient with Madison at times for not getting on with telling Bryce he was a father. Maybe you wondered, along with her, if Bryce was EVER going to grow up. I hope you came to understand, love, and cheer for their little family long before The End.

And now (blink!) we're down to one more Sweet River Ranch romance. You can order Jude and Kaci's story, A Hidden Heiress for the Cowboy, today!

I look forward to seeing you again soon in the log lodge at Sweet River Ranch.

Blessings, Valerie

Psst: Reviews are awesome, too...

ACKNOWLEDGMENTS

Thank you, dear reader, for loving all of the Montana Ranches Christian Romance series: Saddle Springs, Cavanagh Cowboys, and now Sweet River! I'm excited to write the story of the one remaining Sullivan grandson in the next few months.

Thanks to my author buddies Elizabeth Maddrey, Lynnette Bonner, and Jan Thompson for writing sprints and accountability. Friends make such a difference.

My amazing editor, Nicole, has been with me from the beginning. I am so thankful for her!

I'm also grateful for the Christian Indie Authors Facebook group. These folks make a difference in my life every single day. I'm thrilled to walk beside them as we tell stories for Jesus!

Thank you to my Facebook friends, followers, street team, and reader group members for prayers, encouragement, and great fellowship. If you'd like to join other readers who love my stories, please find us at Valerie Comer: Readers Group.

Thanks to my husband, Jim, whose love for me never fails and who encourages me in every endeavor. Thanks to my kids, their spouses, and my wonderful grandkids for cheering me on. To them, having an author for a mom/grandma is "normal." Imagine that!

All my love and gratitude goes to Jesus, the One who is my vision, the High King of Heaven, the lord of my heart. Thank You. A thousand times, thank You.

DEAR READER...

Thanks for reading *A Secret Baby for the Cowboy*! I'm so honored that you chose to spend the last few hours with Bryce, Madison, and me. You are appreciated.

I'm an independent author who relies on my readers to help spread the word about stories you enjoy. Would you take a few minutes to let your friends know? Facebook, Instagram, Goodreads... wherever you hang out online.

Also, each honest review at online retailers means a lot to me and helps other readers know if this is a book they might enjoy. I'd sure appreciate your help getting word out!

I welcome contact from readers. At my website, you can contact me via email, read my blog, and find me on social media. You can also sign up for my newsletter to be notified of new releases, contests, special deals, and more! Click here to subscribe. You'll receive *The Cowboy's Forever Crush*, the novella that introduces all of my Montana Ranches Christian Romance series, absolutely free as my thank you gift!

~ Valerie Comer

www.valeriecomer.com

https://valeriecomer.com/subscribe-crush

BOOKS BY VALERIE COMER

You'll find the complete list of titles by Valerie Comer on her website: fifty books (and counting) in ten series! Come on over to find farm-fresh romance, cowboy romance, and small-town romance, all with distinctly Christian themes.

https://valeriecomer.com/books

ABOUT VALERIE COMER

Valerie Comer is constantly amazed that living, talking, dreaming characters appear in her mind and flow from her fingertips and, from there, to her delighted readers. She only hopes her creations enjoy their happily-ever-afters as much as she does hers, sharing rural life in western Canada with her husband, adult children, and adorable grandkids.

Valerie is a two-time *USA Today* bestselling author and a two-time Word Award winner. She is known for writing engaging characters, strong communities, and deep faith into her green clean romances.

To find out more, visit her website at www.valeriecomer.com, where you can read her blog, explore her many links, and sign up for her email newsletter, where you will find news, giveaways, deals, book recommendations and more. You can also find Valerie blogging with other authors of Christian contemporary romance at Inspy Romance.